A KISS
BEFORE LOVING

A KISS
BEFORE LOVING

MACK REYNOLDS

WILDSIDE PRESS

CHAPTER 1

SHELL HALLIDAY sprawled comfortably in his favorite chair, at his favorite table, at his favorite sidewalk café, the Deux-Magots, on his favorite boulevard, Saint-Germain. His long legs, encased in paint bespattered corduroys, were idly crossed at the ankles and from time to time he got up the energy to do a quick line or two on the sketch pad he held in his lap.

He identified the couple who took the table next to him in a system he had worked out years before. Shirley MacLaine and David Niven. David Niven, say, fifteen years ago. The girl was open of face, animated and friendly. Yes, definitely a Shirley MacLaine type. Probably a Californian. Her escort was undoubtedly British. David Niven playing a stuffy Englishman.

Shell made a quick caricature of him, a line here, a line there, bringing out the stuffiness. A strait-laced British tourist, complete with a somewhat inadequate mustache.

The girl said brightly, "Well, it's Paris. I suppose champagne would be the thing."

Not California, Shell decided. Maybe Florida. Someplace where there was lots of sun and beaches and things like riding water skis behind motorboats. And lots of young people in bathing suits, doing a lot of laughing.

"At this time of day, my dear?" the Englishman said.

Oh, he was stuffy all right.

Shell tightened his lips and shook his head, ever so slightly, at the girl.

She blinked and looked at him, a bit startled.

Using Shell's own system of typing people, she could have thought, *Henry Fonda. Hank Fonda back when he was about twenty-eight or thirty, playing the part of a slow, easygoing artist.*

Shell shifted slightly in his chair and said, "Not champagne here. Maurice will never forgive me for saying so, but not champagne."

"I beg your pardon," the Britisher said, exactly the way, with exactly the inflection, Shell could have predicted.

Shell chose to interpret it as meaning that the other hadn't understood him and wanted a repeat. So Shell said, "I wouldn't order champagne here. It's atrocious."

"Why, you're an American," the girl said.

"That's right."

"You don't look like an American," she said, evidently before thinking.

Shell grinned. "What does an American look like?"

She took in his paint-daubed pants, the beret on his head, the faded corduroy sport jacket. Then she flushed.

Shell laughed and said, "Try the Alsatian Riesling. A bottle of Riesling de Ribeauvillé. Um-m-m, say about nineteen fifty-five. And have them chill it nicely. The Riesling here is excellent."

He returned his attention to his sketching, as though having dismissed them from his mind. The waiter came up and Shell could hear a muttered exchange between the girl and her escort and then the Englishman, in passable French, ordered a bottle of chilled Riesling de Ribeauvillé 1955. By the way he sounded, you could tell he disapproved the selection.

Shell grinned inwardly and made a point of paying them no more attention. He finished the sketch, deciding he'd caught the Britisher rather well.

The wine came, was duly opened and poured into the long-stemmed, tulip-shaped Riesling glasses.

The girl exclaimed, "Why this is wonderful!" and then called over to Shell, "Thank you!"

He looked up. "Eh? Oh, the wine. Is it good?"

"Wonderful. So clean tasting."

"Glad you like it," Shell told her and turned back to his sketch pad.

"Could we offer you a glass?" the girl asked.

Shell frowned, shrugged, came to his feet and, bringing his sketch pad along, made his way to their table. He realized that the girl probably hadn't meant the invitation quite that way, that she could have sent the waiter over with a glass of the wine for him, but Shell chose to interpret her words as an invitation to join them.

The Englishman came to his feet stiffly and made a gesture at one of the two unoccupied chairs.

Shell said, "Thanks," and sat down. He looked at the girl and smiled his easygoing smile. "Shell Halliday," he said.

She smiled in return and said, "Felicity Patterson. Sissy."

He stared at her, his eyes widening.

She laughed. "I wasn't calling you names. I meant, my nickname is Sissy. Everybody calls me Sissy. Felicity just doesn't seem to apply." The corners of her mouth turned down.

Shell laughed, too. "I thought that possibly you were commenting on my wearing a beret. Americans never wear berets, but they're the most comfortable headgear I've come up against." He turned his eyes to the Englishman.

"Brett-James," he volunteered, then hesitated, finally adding, "Michael Brett-James." He had a somewhat high voice.

Shell held out a hand. "Nice to meet you, Mike."

Brett-James winced imperceptibly but shook the proffered hand.

"Shell?" the girl commented. "That's almost as offbeat as my name."

Shell said, "Short for Shelley. Mother has a culture complex. At the time I was born she was going through her poetry period. Later on she was sorry she hadn't named me Rubens or Rembrandt. By that time she was in her painting period."

Sissy Patterson laughed and even Mike Brett-James managed a sour smile.

"Your first trip to Paris, Sissy?" Shell wanted to know. He made a point of first names right off the bat.

"First trip to Europe," she said enthusiastically. "I think it's wonderful. We got to Paris last night. Have you been here long?"

Shell cast his eyes upward in consideration. "I suppose I'm running over four years now."

"Good heavens, haven't you been back to the States at all?"

"Nope. I like it here," Shell said. "Besides, I have the feeling that my work is just getting under way." He added, with a tone of self-deprecation, "I mean that I'm just beginning to *find* myself, sort of reaching a break-through period, you might call it."

She was fascinated. The waiter had brought another glass. She filled it herself. "You know," she said. "I believe you're the first real artist I've ever talked to. I mean a *real* artist."

Shell said, "No different from anybody else."

"No, I mean *really*. Bohemian and everything. An artist living and working in Paris. I'd just *love* to see some of your work."

"Sissy, we should be running along, you know," Brett-James cut in. "We've got to dress for dinner." He was obviously unhappy about the manner in which Shell had moved in upon them.

Sissy ignored him. She said to Shell, "Four years. Good Heavens, you must know Paris like a book."

He shrugged. "As a matter of fact, I guess I have seen quite a bit of the real Paris." He pursed his lips. "Discovering the real Paris, the inner Paris, you might call it, takes a bit of doing." He turned his eyes to Brett-James. "Where were you figuring on eating, Mike?"

From the Englishman's expression, Shell might have just asked him whether or not his sister was a virgin. He sputtered a moment before saying, "Why, we have reservations at Maxim's."

Shell said nothing to that.

Sissy filled his glass again, looked around for the waiter and, American style, made a circular motion with her hand to indicate the desire for another bottle of the Riesling. She turned back to Shell and asked, "What's the matter with Maxim's? It's the most famous restaurant in the world, isn't it? I even saw it in a movie once."

"It's famous, all right," Shell said. "Three stars in Michelin. You can't get a higher restaurant rating than that. Maxim's, Tour d'Argent, Grand Vefour, Lapérouse, Escargot-Montorgueil—the best restaurants in the world. You should give them a try." He made a gesture with his right hand, rocking it back and forth as though in negation. "However …"

Sissy was listening, wide-eyed, fascinated.

"Well … what?" she prodded.

"I don't know. We were talking about the *real* Paris a moment ago. Not the tourist Paris. Not the ultra-expensive Paris." He seemed lost in thought for a moment. "Not even the Frenchman's Paris, because Paris isn't just a French city. It's the city of light, the city of art—it's the city of every man, every nationality that loves art."

"Good Heavens," Sissy Patterson said, meaninglessly. She poured more wine.

Brett-James looked at his watch impatiently.

Sissy ignored him. "Look here, Shell," she said. "Now don't say no before I finish." She slapped the table with the flat of her palm, definitely. "I want you to take Mike and me to dinner." She added quickly, "On me, of course. I insist on paying for everything."

"Oh now, Sissy—" Mike started.

She turned to him. "No, Mike, I mean it. Good Heavens, we can go to that stuffy old Maxim's any time at all. But this is our chance. Shell here is a real Bohemian. I told you I wanted to meet some real Bohemians, and I'm not going to have you ruin it, Mike Brett-James."

Brett-James cast his eyes heavenwards, the first human thing Shell had seen him do thus far.

Shell laughed uncomfortably. "That word Bohemian is somewhat elastic."

She was insistent. "Take us someplace where you … well, suppose you had just sold a painting or something and were going to celebrate and money meant nothing. That's what I want to do. And later, oh please, could you take us around to … well, you know … some of these places where the real artists go … in cellars and everything."

Shell hesitated, as though trying to find words to deny her.

"Now don't you say no," she followed up quickly. "I don't think it would be too much to take a fellow American around as a favor once in a while. You've had the advantage of living here for years and if you ever came to Palm City, I'd be glad to—"

She stopped suddenly and flushed. "I'm sorry," she said. "Possibly you have a date or something." Her voice turned miserable. "I get so enthusiastic about things and make a jerk of myself every time."

Mike Brett-James cleared his throat and came to his feet, looking for the waiter.

Shell snapped his fingers decisively. "Why not? I've been working too hard. I could use a night on the town. We'll have fun."

"Oh, wonderful," Sissy breathed.

"It's a deal," Shell said.

The waiter came and Shell said idly, "Maurice, just put this on my bill."

"Oh no, you don't," Sissy said quickly. "Give me that check. This is my party, and neither of you boys is going to pay a thing."

She opened her bag and brought forth a fistful of one hundred denomination francs. "Is this enough?" she said. "I don't understand this money very well."

Maurice grimaced in pain, took up a single bill and went off for change.

Shell laughed and said, "One of those is about twenty dollars, Sissy."

She said hopelessly, "I have no idea of money. I have a hard time keeping track of even American money."

* * * *

Shell acquired a cab after no more than the average effort involved in hailing a taxi in Paris, and gave the driver directions. They took off in a stomach-chilling clash of gears and slammed into the traffic.

"Oh, this is going to be wonderful," Sissy gushed.

Mike Brett-James said protestingly, "I say, aren't we even going to go back to the hotel to change?"

Shell grinned at him. "Mike, we're going to one of the best bistros, in Paris, but it's absolutely undiscovered so far as the tourist hordes are concerned. Here in the Latin Quarter, it's top secret. You know, classified. However ..."

"Good Heavens," Sissy said deliciously.

"... I doubt if there's ever been a party in dinner dress in the place. I'd hate to set the precedent. The gang would have me out and lined up against the wall at the Invalides." He dropped the banter. "I hope you like Burgundian food. Robert is from Lyon."

"Of course," Mike said stiffly.

"Oh, yes," Sissy breathed.

Shell said, "Frog legs and snails are particular Burgundian delicacies."

Sissy sucked in her breath.

Shell laughed at her. "I was kidding you," he said. "As a matter of fact, their snails are tops but you don't have to try them."

Sissy said, "I've had frog legs. Goodness, the best frog legs in the world come from out of the Everglades."

"You'll have to try Robert's," Shell told her.

Their careening cab, obviously driven by a suicidal maniac, shot suddenly off to the right and onto a smaller street than Boulevard Saint-Germain.

"This is Rue Monsieur Le Prince," Shell told them. "Lots of students at the Sorbonne live in the neighborhood. Back before my paintings began to go fairly well, I used to stay here. You can get a room for as little as a dollar a day."

"Must be terrible," Mike protested.

"A little on the grim side," Shell admitted. "But fun."

"I can *imagine*," Sissy said.

They went on a little beyond the Rue Casimir DeLavigne and the cab came to a halt in a snarling of brakes. The driver relaxed and settled back for all the world as though he had never really expected to make it.

They climbed out and Shell reached in his pocket for money, saying in a sour voice in English to the driver, "Wow, how many more lessons before you get a license?"

"Eh, Monsieur?"

Sissy was laughing. "No, no," she protested. "You promised. Everything is on me. Otherwise, I'd just never feel right about ... well, kidnapping you like this." She fumbled in her bag for money for the taxi.

Shell shrugged. "I feel like a kept man," he said. Then he added as an after thought, "You know, it feels good, for a change."

Mike Brett-James didn't join them in the laughter but they swept together up to the less than imposing door. The Britisher scowled at it. "You're sure this is the place?"

"Never judge a Parisian restaurant by its entry," Shell told him. "For that matter, even your Maxim's looks like a second-rate American hash house—from outside."

They entered, and whether or not Maxim's exterior looked like a hash house, certainly the interior of Robert's did. The smells that wafted about the room were exotic, however.

"I say," Brett-James protested. "Miss Patterson would hardly—"

"Oh, do be quiet, Mike," Sissy said.

An aristocratic, high-nosed character came sweeping up. An Eric Blore type, Shell Halliday had decided long ago. Eric Blore in his best role as butler or headwaiter.

"Monsieur Halliday," this one gushed. *"Bon soir! Comment—?"*

Shell held up a hand. *"Anglais, s'il vous plaît, Robert.* My friends speak English."

Robert switched without a second's hesitation. "But you have been avoiding us. We have been desolate. This very afternoon Pierre was saying the *saupiquet montbardois* was a creation today and that it would be tragic if you did not dine with us."

"Good Heavens, what's that?" Sissy whispered.

Shell chuckled. "A piquant sauce the chef here is a master at." He said to Robert, "I'm sorry I didn't make reservations. It was a last-moment decision."

The headwaiter made a Gallic gesture with his hands and a toss of his head. "We can always find room for a party of yours, Monsieur Halliday." He turned his beaming face to Sissy and Mike Brett-James.

"Robert, this is Miss Patterson and Mister Brett-James," Shell said. "Mind them well. And do me proud tonight. I have expressed the opinion that Robert's is currently the outstanding undiscovered restaurant in all Paris."

Robert bowed sweepingly and led them to as good a table as was still unoccupied. He swept the reservation sign away and helped them into their chairs.

He snapped his fingers for a waiter and took their order himself. Evidently, in Robert's there were no menus. Instead, he and Shell chattered back and forth in French for the next ten or fifteen minutes. From time to time Shell would consult with them.

"He says that the *quenelles de brochet au beurre d'écrevisses* are excellent this evening. That's a sort of pike fishball deal with a sauce of fresh cream and crayfish butter."

"I know what it is," Mike said in irritation. He was on the edge of rebellion at the whole situation.

"Good Heavens," Sissy said, "it sounds marvelous. You decide, Shell."

"And the *pauchouse de la Saône*. That's a kind of stew of freshwater fish seasoned with herbs and onions and Burgundy wine. I can recommend it highly."

"You decide," Sissy repeated.

Brett-James put in a few comments by way of not allowing himself to be completely eclipsed, but largely the ordering was in Shell's obviously competent hands. When all was done, he asked Robert to send over the *sommelier* and once again it was a lengthy matter involving a Chablis of good year for the fish course, a Red Romanée-Conti with the entree, to wind up at last with a champagne for the cheese.

"No martini while we're waiting?" Sissy asked.

Mike Brett-James was able to take over at last. "My dear, they'd drum us from the building if we drank a cocktail before dinner in a French restaurant."

"But I had one last night at the Ritz Bar."

Mike said distastefully, "The Ritz is more American than the Waldorf in New York. They'd sell you a drink of paraffin there, if you requested it."

"Paraffin?"

"We Americans call it kerosene," Shell told her. "The French won't smoke or drink strong liquor before meals. They figure it kills the palate. They're right, of course."

"I like a few drinks before eating," Sissy said. It was the first objection she'd made thus far. She'd been like a four-year-old in a candy shop.

Making idle conversation, Shell said, "You people known each other very long?"

Brett-James stared at him coldly, as though he'd pulled a *faux pas*. Shell ignored him and looked at Sissy.

"Oh, no. I landed at Gibraltar, oh, a week or two ago. I had some friends of friends, like, up the coast in Torremolinos. Do you know Torremolinos?"

"Heard of it," Shell murmured. "Some of the gang go down in August to escape the heat here."

"Well, it's quite a spot. The new art colony. Parties day and night. Anyway, I met Mike there at—whose party was it, Mike?"

"Princess Bourbon-Palma," Mike said stiffly.

"That's right. A real princess. It was lots of fun, but I've wanted to see Paris for ever so long and, well, Torremolinos isn't much different from Florida."

The soup and the Chablis arrived and Sissy gushed some more.

She could evidently knock it back, Shell Halliday decided wryly. They went through two bottles before the fish was finished.

By the time the champagne arrived and had been well sampled, none of them were feeling any strain. Even Mike had loosened up a bit, although he still obviously viewed Shell as an intruder on his evening. Finally, Sissy remembered that they were to do a round of the *chansonniers, caves*, and the more intimate bistros, and called rather loudly for the check.

Robert himself came and presented it to Shell.

Sissy said, indignantly, "No, no, this is my party," and took it out of Shell's hand.

"Monsieur Halliday," Robert said. "Pierre, the chef, would be disconsolate if you left without saying a word."

Shell came to his feet and excused himself for a moment. "I wanted to congratulate him anyway," he told Robert. "The *boeuf bourguignon* was as good as any I've ever tasted."

Back in the passageway that led to the kitchen, Shell waited until Robert came up. The headwaiter put a hand in his pocket and came out with a sheaf of bills. "It came to three hundred and twenty francs," Robert said in businesslike tone. "Ten per cent gives you thirty-two francs."

Shell pocketed the money. "Look, they'll probably be coming back on their own," he said.

Robert made with a Gallic shrug. "If so, I'll remember and perhaps give you a bonus," he said. "The agreement is that you get your percentage only when you accompany a party. If they return on their own, that's another matter."

Shell grumbled, "At Vezelay's they give me a cut on every meal a customer buys, if I introduce him in the first place."

Robert said evenly, "Vezelay's is a pigsty. Here one dines well. Our cuisine is such that the bill cannot be padded to make up your percentage."

Shell grunted a response and returned to the table.

He shook his head wryly. "That Pierre is a character. I've been half kiddingly trying to talk him into going over to the States. He'd make a fortune there. He's horrified at the idea. He's heard about such things as catsup and putting fruit in salad."

Sissy came to her feet, slightly wobbly. Brett-James frowned at her but was obviously feeling no pain himself.

* * * *

They did the town up brown.

Violins by the dozen at the Monseigneur, on Rue d'Amsterdam. Sissy's eyes shone with champagne and reflected glamour, as two score White Russians surrounded their tables and drowned all possible conversation. When the musicians had drifted on, she caught her breath. "Why, this place is like a jewel box."

Shell chuckled. "And it'll take a fistful of jewels to pay the bill, too. One of the most expensive spots in town."

"Oh, the money isn't anything. Good Heavens, this is fabulous."

Strip-teasers by the dozen at the Drap d'Or, complete with audience participation. Sissy giggled gleefully as the red-faced Mike Brett-James did his best to undress the pert little brunette who perched on his knees, rumpled his hair, nibbled his ear, as he worked away at buttons and snaps, to the hilarity of the clientele. He had obviously been picked as the most strait-laced-looking man present.

Carroll's, where the sexes are three—at least. And where you have to flip a coin to decide if the waitress is a waitress or a waiter. And Madame Arthur's, where the waiters are waiters more or less, but are dressed like waitresses.

At Le Monocle, where there was dancing, with ultra-masculine-appearing women paired off with ultra-feminine bits of fluff. Sissy watched wide-eyed, while Brett-James sat stiffly in dignified protest and Shell yawned.

She said, "You know, I've heard about these places but—well, I never really believed ..." Her sentence dribbled away.

Shell grinned at her. "Never believed what?"

Sissy said, "Well, good Heavens, look at the pretty little thing over there. The one with the red hair. She's looking up at that partner of hers with a swooning look like ... well, like it was a man."

"It damn near is," Shell chuckled.

Sissy said suddenly, "It makes me feel ... funny. Mike, let's dance."

The Britisher protested. "Here? With all those, ah, women? I'd feel conspicuous, my dear. Why don't we leave?"

Sissy's eyes turned to Shell. "You'll dance with me. I suddenly feel like I want a *man's* arms around me."

Shell was on his feet. He bowed sweepingly. "A privilege, and thanks for the compliment."

Mike Brett-James looked as though he wanted to say something, but couldn't quite think of it.

Evidently, looking at the Sapphic clientele of Le Monocle had brought something out in Sissy Patterson—a need to emphasize her own obvious femininity. On the dance floor, she pressed close to him. Her full breasts were obvious, through her dress, her warm and full hips obviously those of a live, vibrant woman. The thought touched Shell's mind that in this warm weather, the girl was probably wearing the barest minimum beneath her dress. They danced close on the crowded floor, and Shell wondered if she was so far gone in the drinking and excitement of the evening that she failed to recognize his own masculine reaction to the closeness of her body.

He said into her ear, "Realize that possibly we're the only two normal people on this floor?"

She looked up at him, coyly, enticingly, and murmured, "Well, there's no denying you come under that category."

He decided Sissy Patterson was an exciting woman, and that it might pay to get better acquainted.

Tiring of the depressing queerness of the homo joints, they left for the Pigalle section.

Les Naturistes. The Sphinx. L'Indifférent. Chez Eve.

After one of the frankest dance-team acts that any of the three of them had ever seen performed, Shell said dryly, "That wraps its up. There is only one thing left they could do as an encore."

Sissy dissolved in laughter.

Sissy was having herself a time. It was no longer champagne. She'd switched to Scotch and she ordered it by the bottle. Shell Halliday estimated she'd go about a hundred and twenty, dripping wet, but brother she could knock it back. She was certainly putting away as much as either he or Brett-James, and not showing as much effect. Face it, she was drinking twice as much as the Britisher, and Mike was reeling.

She had lost all track of the money she was spending. Certainly she'd dropped several hundred dollars. In one of the Pigalle joints alone, the manager had slipped Shell fifty francs—ten bucks. It was a clip joint, and Shell got twenty per cent there, which meant that she'd spent fifty dollars, and it had been only a brief stop.

Shell shook his head. She was really something. You had to keep your eye on her. When she'd said, earlier, that she had no idea about money, she wasn't just whistling Dixie. She'd given one waiter a hundred-franc tip, mistaking the bill for a ten. In joints where the service charge was already twenty per cent, she'd tip another ten or twenty. Twice she left her bag behind. Cleanly forgot it. If Shell hadn't been there and as well known as he was, she'd never have seen it again. He shuddered at the thought of the routine you have to go through to get a new passport and to try and collect on lost travelers' checks.

Sissy impressed Shell. She was as good-natured a tourist as he'd run into in the past three years. She was loving every moment of it and was obviously as hot as a firecracker. As Brett-James, her supposed escort, fell further and further into an alcoholic daze, she diverted her attention to Shell. A touch of a toe tip against his leg beneath the table, more of the close dancing they'd had at Le Monocle, an occasional pressure of the hand, a provocative glance now and then.

This Brett-James was another kettle of fish. As they traveled up a one-way street Shell tried to figure him. Obviously, old school tie type of Englishman, the kind who was more British than Churchill. But there was something off key. Shell couldn't put his finger on it. The Britisher had started off the evening resenting Shell rather openly, but as he got increasingly stoned, the antagonism dropped away, although it must have been obvious that Shell and Sissy were reacting to each other.

They were back on the Left Bank again, in the early hours, sitting at a miniature table in Gordon Payant's little *cave*. The American Negro was singing folksongs in a half dozen different languages. He was currently the most popular entertainer in the St. Germain des Prés section and Shell got no rake-off here. Which was all right with him. He'd already made enough tonight to last him a week or more and he and Payant knew and liked each other.

A German peasant song ended and the clients, jam-packed in the little room, began snapping their fingers by way of applause.

Sissy said, "What's that?"

"The snapping-fingers bit?" Shell said. "It started down on the Riviera. Gordon had a place there in a residential section of town and the neighbors complained about the noise at night. So they established the custom of snapping fingers instead of clapping hands in the way of applause. When Gordon moved up here he brought the custom along."

Somebody came bustling up to their table, frisking cocker spaniel style. It was Dave Shepherd.

"Why Shell, dear boy. Haven't seen you for *ages*."

"Hi. Sit down for a minute," he suggested.

"Hello, Mike," Dave simpered. "Dear boy, I didn't know you were in Gay Paree!" He turned back to Shell. "Well, just for a *moment*. I'm with the baroness and her party."

Shell didn't ask what baroness. If he had, Dave probably would have told them in lengthy detail, going back through the family titles to the fifteenth generation. Dave Shepherd was the only person Shell had ever met who read *Burke's Peerage* as though it were current literature.

Mike Brett-James had flinched slightly when Dave greeted him but he said, "How are you, David?"

"David Shepherd, this is Miss Felicity Patterson," Shell made the introduction. "Dave is the town crier, Sissy. Knows everything that happens in Paris and tells all to all."

Dave made a limp motion of his left hand as though to slap Shell. "Oh, *you*," he said. He looked at Sissy.

"Have a drink," Sissy invited.

"Why, I don't really have time, my dear," Dave said. "Patterson? Of the Rhode Island Pattersons, of course."

"No," Sissy said briefly, the sides of her mouth turning down. "Florida."

"So you know Mike, eh? Small world, the international set," Shell said.

"Oh dear, yes. For *ever* so many years. Where was it we first met, dear boy?"

Mike Brett-James said uncomfortably, "At the pension the Contessa Clara Rossi had near Nice. You were staying there at the time. I stopped for a weekend."

"What a *lovely* memory you have."

Shell laughed. "That's the first time I've ever heard that adjective applied to memory," he said.

Dave came to his feet. "I simply must go," he gushed. "I'll see all you *charming* people later. 'Bye-'bye." He frisked off.

Shell thought, an Alan Ladd type, if Ladd had a part playing a queer. But it'd be a hard role to put over. Almost a caricature.

"Is he … well … you know, that way?" Sissy asked.

Shell laughed. "Dave is as far that way as he can go without falling off the edge."

She looked after him. "Good Heavens, he'd be a handsome man if—"

"—if he was a man," Shell finished. "Look, children, the time has come to finish it all off with a visit to Les Halles."

Sissy was all for it. "Where's that?" she said. "More fun than here?"

Mike rallied enough to say. "It's the big market. It just gets under full swing this time of morning. I haven't been there for a donkey's years, but it's fascinating. Call it the Belly of Paris."

Sissy was surprised. "But what would we want to go to a market for?"

"For onion soup," Shell told her.

"Yes, that's true," Brett-James nodded solemnly. "Tradition, you know. Onion soup at Les Halles after a night on Paris." Mike looked as though he could use something to counter the load he was carrying.

"Sounds horrible," Sissy said gaily, "but let's go."

Their taxi zoomed across the Seine at the Pont Neuf and headed for the Halles markets. To their left loomed the Louvre, a massive shadow in the darkness of the night. Like all Parisian cabbies, the driver careened through the streets as though a posse was after them.

Traffic had fallen off and for a brief few blocks the streets were quiet and gray. And then, suddenly, they were in a bedlam, a madhouse, a noisy, confused, chaotic asylum of pushcarts, trucks, horse-drawn wagons and yelling, shouting, sometimes screaming, men and women. Crates of fruit, vegetables, poultry; sides of beef, sheep, pigs, goats. Barrels of wine, cases of beer, rounds of cheese, endless links of a thousand varieties of sausage.

"Good Heavens," Sissy said.

"Les Halles," Shell said. He leaned forward to the driver. "*A la Au Pied de Cochon, s'il vous plaît.*"

They pulled up before the market restaurant, paid off the taxi and wove their way in. The place was jam-packed with market workers standing at the bar, overflowing the tables. Shell led them to the stairs and to the second floor where they managed to find a table. Here, incongruously, was the atmosphere of a first-class restaurant, fine linen, excellent lighting, waiters as well turned out as those in the deluxe establishments.

"The specialties are onion soup and grilled pigs' feet, and wonderful for sobering-up purposes." Shell told Sissy.

"I'm not sure I want to sober up," she said petulantly. She looked at Brett-James, "And I'm sure Mike doesn't."

"Wha…?" was Mike's only comment.

"You'll bless me in the morning," Shell told them. He was conscious of her foot, under the table, touching his and rubbing.

By the time they left, the first dirty streaks of dawn were beginning to gray the skies. Shell bundled them into another cab. "Where to?" he asked Sissy.

"Wherever you say," she said. "I'm game."

He laughed at her. "I meant, where's your hotel? Onion soup at Les Halles marks the end of a night on the town in Paris."

There was disappointment in her voice. "Well, the Ritz," she said.

"Mike?" Shell asked.

But Mike was asleep.

"He's at the Lancaster, I think," Sissy said. "He said his family always stays there."

"I know where it is," Shell said. "We'll deliver you first, and then I'll see he gets back to his place."

He left Mike snoring in the cab and saw her to the door of her suite. She looked up into his face and her mouth was slack, her eyes almost closed.

Shell swallowed and licked his lower lip. "Look," he said. "I'll have to get Mike back to his hotel."

"Of course. Good night, Shell. I've never had such fun." Aside from a slight slur, you'd never know the girl had the better part of a fifth of Scotch in her, not to speak of the dinner wines and liqueurs. She looked at him invitingly and said, looking him in the eye, "Up to this point, this is exactly the way I've always dreamed Paris would be."

Suddenly, she leaned against him, raised her arms, placed them around his neck and put her mouth to his, her hot tongue darting quickly in and out. The next moment she had released him and was gone, closing the door behind her. Shell stared hard at the door before he left abruptly.

* * * *

At the curb, before the open door of the cab, Shell turned and looked back at the ornate entrance of the Ritz with its marble and woodwork. He ran his tongue over his lower lip again, then climbed in and told the driver, *"Le Lancaster, 7 Rue de Berri, s'il vous plaît."*

The doorman at the Lancaster helped him with Mike Brett-James and then a bellhop and an elevator operator did their bit toward getting his charge to his room. Someone, along the line, had accumulated the Englishman's door key.

Mike woke briefly and in a blur while Shell was undressing him, preparatory to putting him into bed. He leered at Shell slyly. Good grief, the man wore long underwear. Shell couldn't remember having seen the garment for twenty years. His grandfather, back in Ohio, was the last American he'd ever seen in "long-handled underwear" as the old boy used to call it.

The Englishman awoke only long enough to tell Shell it was a long way to Tipperary and to demand to be kissed good night. When Shell didn't comply he went on back to sleep. To hell with finding his pajamas, Shell decided. Let him sleep in his woolen longies.

He had told the cab to wait. Now he took it and retraced his route. There had been invitation in Sissy's kiss and he had every intention of taking her up on it.

He paid the driver off, hesitated only momentarily and then entered the hotel. He spoke briefly at the desk, then took the elevator.

Surprisingly, he found himself eager to get back to her—to take up where they had left off. That, in itself, made him wonder because it had been a long time since he'd felt this way.

At her door, he knocked.

Sissy opened it, somewhat sleepy of eye. She obviously hadn't been to bed, although she was in a negligee of the texture of woven spider thread, so revealing as to be almost nonexistent.

She looked at him, one eyebrow slightly higher than the other.

Shell held up her purse. "You left it in the cab," he said.

"Oh," she said, almost whispering it and then went on, "I wondered what excuse you'd find."

"I beg your pardon?" Shell said, following her into the room.

"I've made a couple of drinks for us, as nightcaps," she went on, turning to him.

He was already thinking, *Wow, what a night. I've made plenty—much better than usual—it's been fun, with the exception of the wet blanket, Brett-James, and now ... this. That negligee must have cost a fortune and it conceals absolutely nothing. This girl has an unbelievable figure.*

The nightcaps were sitting on a cocktail table. Mike bent to pick one up, turning away from her momentarily. When he turned back, Sissy had allowed the negligee to part, revealing two halves of proud, almost arrogant breasts.

Without taking his eyes off her, Shell placed the drink back on the cocktail table. Sissy, satisfied with the effect her strip-tease was having, thrust one leg forward, separating the negligee further to expose a restless, well-rounded thigh. Then, with one quick move, she squirmed, shrugged her shoulders and the negligee wafted rather than slid down her body and settled to the floor.

Now she walked to him deliberately, flaunting every inch of her manificent figure, her breasts bouncing in rhythm to her stride. For the second time that evening she thrust herself at him, threw her arms around his neck and urged, "Now show me how they make love in Paris."

They never got around to their drinks.

CHAPTER 2

SHELL WOKE FIRST. From the light streaming through the large windows, it must have been somewhat after noon, he figured. For a brief moment he had to orientate himself—a slight hangover … last night on the town … the American girl and the Englishman …

It all came back in a rush.

He turned on his side. Her hair, against the white of the other pillow was dark gold. He remembered her strip-tease of the night before and the way she had urged him to greater and greater ecstasy.

Shell Halliday decided that Sissy Patterson was one of the few women he'd met who looked better completely nude than in clothing. Contrary to considerable belief, complete nudity is seldom as attractive as when a woman wears some minimum of clothing, a thin nightgown, a bikini, or even a G-string in a strip-tease. Once the last article of provocative clothing is shed, the mystery is gone.

But this girl had such a perfect collection of feminine attributes that the generalization just didn't apply.

She lay now in such a way that her body was evident from the navel up, and her face was serene in sleep, as though she'd never dreamed of alcoholic indulgence beyond some slight sipping of Aunt Minnie's blackberry wine, come Thanksgiving, and was as virginal as all seven of the Vestals.

Only a sheet covered her. The night before had been warm and their exertions hadn't cooled it. With deliberation, Shell stretched forth a hand and gently pulled the sheet away. Yes, her feet, calves, knees, thighs and hips were as perfect as he had remembered them, and he remembered them well. She was a Venus de Milo, with several inches added to her breast measurements to bring her up to modern American specifications.

Felicity Patterson had an attractive face, but her surpassing beauty was in her figure. Shell extended a finger toward a nipple so coral as to be suspect of cosmetic addition.

Sissy opened one eye and frowned at him.

"You're awfully forward for a comparative stranger," she said accusingly.

He grinned at her, unabashed. "I'm not as strange as all that," he said.

"You're pretty strange," she said. "Where'd you learn some of those things you did to me last night?"

"What things?"

"You know." She brought the sheet up around her neck and brought her arms tight against her body and shivered slightly. "Scary. But not at the time, of course."

He pretended to leer. "You're not so bad yourself."

"Humph," she said, "I come by my experience honestly, through two marriages. While I have a sneaking suspicion that you've accumulated yours by picking up poor little tourist waifs who have lost their way in Paris—and taking them off and seducing them."

"Them's harsh words," Shell protested. He felt a comfortable languor and was unprepared for the bombshell that came.

Sissy had put one of her hands behind her head and was staring up at the ceiling. After a moment she said, as though idly, "You could have kept the purse, you know. We probably spent quite a bit last night, but I imagine there's a couple of thousand dollars in francs, dollars and pounds in it."

He couldn't have been more surprised had she suddenly ground her cigarette into his face.

"What?" he said.

She knew he had heard her correctly.

"What brought that on?" he wanted to know after a pause. "Do you think I'm a crook?"

She looked at him obliquely, drew on her cigarette again. "What are you, Shell?"

He said indignantly, "You know what I am. I'm an American painter, living here in Paris."

She said softly, "Do you really do any painting?"

His eyes pried at her.

"I'm not as scatterbrained as I sometimes seem," she said. "Oh, I'm scatterbrained, I'll admit, but not completely stupid."

"What's all that mean?" Shell snapped.

"It didn't mean so much at Robert's when you went in to have a word with Pierre, the chef. By the way, is there really a chef there named Pierre?"

"Yes," Shell said flatly.

"But in the next place there was also a reason to go off with the head-waiter for a moment, after the check had been paid. Then the third time."

"And …?" Shell said.

Sissy yawned. "And then I stopped paying any attention."

"Look," he said bitterly. "Why didn't you call it quits if that's what you thought?"

She looked at him. "Why? I was having the time of my life. Your company is excellent. You really do know Paris. Why should I object to paying for your guide services?"

"And my gigolo services afterwards, eh?" he muttered.

She flushed. "That was uncalled for."

She was right, damn it. Shell Halliday was sorry he had dragged that in. "You're right," he said grudgingly. "I apologize. As for the rest, you're right, of course. I get a percentage for bringing tourists into most of those places we were in last night."

Sissy shrugged her shapely shoulders. "So you earn your money. At least, your way of making a living is more honest than mine. I don't do anything."

He frowned at her.

Sissy laughed sourly. "I have a trust that nets me a thousand a week. My father knew that if he left me his money in a chunk I'd probably get done out of it before the year was through. So he left a trust. A thousand a week. I have a hard time getting rid of it, Shell."

He grunted and stared up at the ceiling. "At least, your father made it," he said. "If he wanted to leave it to you, that's his business. He wasn't a bum living off tourists, a steerer, a shill, a tout."

"Hey, laddy," she said, her voice suddenly compassionate. She turned to him and took him in her arms, as though she were twenty years older, and he twenty younger. Suddenly she was eternal womanhood, protecting a male-child, soul-hurt by a less than clement world.

She kissed him passionlessly on his forehead. "You're too young to be bitter, laddy." There was a tender quality in the girl which amazed him. His snap judgments of the evening before—and the night—melted away.

He snorted in self-deprecation. "Thanks, Sissy. You're a nice guy."

"Almost everybody does the best they can, laddy, including you. You're a nice guy, too."

He snorted again but said nothing.

She was stroking his head gently. "Want me to scratch your back?"

That surprised him. "How did you know I like to have my back scratched?"

She laughed gently. "All little boys like to have their backs scratched."

He was unaccountably uncomfortable with this new Sissy. He didn't feel that he wanted this sort of thing, this *real* intimacy from one of his tourist pickups. He wanted to bring the thing back to their earlier flippancy. She was capable of giving, and was giving, more than he wished to take—from any woman. There was a certain strength he could find in his bitterness— and she was robbing him of that bitterness.

He pulled her to him roughly, wanting to hurt her for daring to invade his innermost privacy. He cupped one of her lush breasts in his hand. Almost instantly, the nipple hardened beneath his palm and his mood changed abruptly.

He pressed closer and she could evidently feel his maleness against her since an expression at once tense and still sensually slack passed over her face. She moaned, "Good Heavens, you're amazingly virile," and her eyes rolled upward.

Shell reacted in surprise. He had never met a woman who responded so quickly, whose needs were so immediate.

That one hand over her breast turned on an excitement that was as intense as it was real. Her mouth sought his immediately, her tongue brazen, inviting and demanding more intimacies.

Shell ignored the urgency of her need, anxious to dwell for a time on provocative preliminaries, both hands now caressing her breasts with a feathery touch which made Sissy gasp with pleasure.

"Laddy, laddy," she cooed, "you've got it made, you've got it made ..."

The rebellion in him was fading fast, but its residue made him hold off. He felt, somehow—despite his own need for the ultimate intimacy—that he had to make her wait and, perhaps, even beg.

His right hand slid down her breast, traced its way down the now quivering slope of her belly and then stroked an inner thigh, again with that feathery touch which had forced words from Sissy before.

She shook as if with fever and her arms drew him down onto her as she moaned, "Goddamnit! I can't wait another second—not another goddamn second ..."

Her voice trailed off into a whimper as she shifted her position to accommodate him ... Before all thoughts were swept away in their passion, the last thought he was conscious of was: *Is this girl a nympho, or a near one?* She was as wildly Lilith now as, a moment before, she had been eternal Eve.

After the tidal wave of climax, they relaxed with their cigarettes, comfortably and warmly close, but not touching at any body area. They watched their smoke ascend through the unstirring air, toward the highly decorative ceiling.

Finally, she said softly, "Before we so beautifully interrupted our conversation, you were belaboring yourself about your method of making a living. Do you know how my father made his?"

"No, of course not." He wondered vaguely what difference it made.

"He was the biggest bootlegger in Florida during Prohibition," she said evenly. "After repeal, he was well established in the liquor business and became the biggest distributor in the Deep South."

What could he say to that? Shell frowned but remained silent. It was nothing to beat herself about. The way her father made his money wasn't her responsibility.

"You know all those old saws: *Money won't buy everything, Crime doesn't pay*, and *Honesty is the best policy*, that sort of thing? Well, I'll tell you something, Shell. You know why they lasted long enough to become old saws? Because as corny as they might sound to wise-acre cynics like you and I think we are, they're true. They're true, Shell."

"True or not," he said sourly, "I doubt if I'd turn down a thousand a week if somebody handed it to me. I don't think I'd spend time thinking how the money had been made."

She remained quiet for a long moment. "No, I suppose not," she sighed. "I probably sound like a fool to you, Shell." She turned on her side, propped herself on her elbow and frowned down at him.

"I'm twenty-eight years old, Shell. You know what my score is? Two husbands, two divorces, and one nine-year-old child. If I had to count the number of persons I can truly consider to be real friends—those not just interested in my money—I could do it on one hand and have several fingers left over."

She grunted self-derision. "As you've discovered, I like men. My appetites are normal and I'm not quite thirty, so why shouldn't I? I like masculine companionship, and not just in bed. I'm a born wife. I like to cook. Believe it or not, Shell, I even like to do things like sew buttons on men's shirts. I like the smell of a man around the house. You know, pipes and things." She snorted self-contempt again.

"That shouldn't be hard for a girl like you to—" he started to say.

"Even in Florida, the daughters of men who become rich by bootlegging aren't exactly acceptable in the best circles," she cut in wearily. "I suppose Dad thought he could take care of that situation as I grew older. Well, he learned his lessons as I learned mine." Her mouth twisted without humor. "I remember his taking me to a top girls' school in Maryland. They'd accepted me by mail."

Shell was looking at her narrowly. He saw that no comment was expected from him.

"Evidently, the old biddy in charge had checked further on our background. They couldn't have been more gentle about it, but suddenly there was no room for Felicity Patterson. The school was full up."

She grimaced again. "Dad was furious. He wanted to buy the place and fire all the snobs running it. What he probably really wanted to do was send some of his heavies up to deal with this problem as he'd dealt with all the others in his career." She shrugged. "Obviously, that's not an answer. I found out there was no answer."

She remained quiet for a moment, then wound it up quickly, as though tired of the subject. "So when you grow up, you kind of automatically drift into the hard-drinking, sleeping-around set. My first husband was a bartender. The second was, supposedly, a movie star. Actually, he turned out to be a bit player. Even that was *before* he married the Felicity Patterson fortune. He stopped working entirely, afterward. He was the father of Bunny."

"Bunny?"

"My daughter. She's in a school in Switzerland now."

Shell wondered why in the world she was giving all this to him. But, in a way, he supposed he knew. You have to talk to somebody. Sooner or later, you have to talk to somebody. And why not him? At least, Shell wouldn't repeat it to anybody who made any difference.

And there was another angle. If you want compassion, go to those who have their own troubles. Go to the poor and the beaten by life, if you want sympathy. Those who have suffered themselves know how it is. Sissy probably sensed that Shell's own life hadn't exactly been a boundless success.

"Sorry, kid. It sounds rugged," he said softly.

She stubbed her cigarette out, as though defiantly. "I talk to much," she said.

"What're you doing in Europe, Sissy?" Shell asked, his voice gentle.

She laughed suddenly, and her laugh was bitterly harsh. "Looking for Number Three—a husband." She added, sharply, "Bunny needs a father. A father and a normal home life. Let's get up, Shell. I could use some breakfast."

* * * *

The Ritz is centrally located at 15 Place Vendôme. When Shell Halliday eventually emerged into the square, the day was well into afternoon. He looked up at the statue of Napoleon there at the top of the bronze pillar made of captured enemy cannon—Napoleon in the toga of a Roman emperor and with a laurel wreath on his head. In such garb, the little corporal looked ludicrous.

The day was such as only Paris in early summer can provide. Shell decided to walk back to his own hotel. Among other things, he wanted to think. Sissy had brought on a mood of recapitulation.

He strolled down Rue Castiglione toward the Tuileries gardens, hands in pockets.

What was it she'd said? He could have kept the purse, there was probably several thousand dollars in it.

Actually, it had never occurred to him. But had he taken it, she would have made no effort to apprehend him. And even if he had, there would have been no proof. Sissy had shown that with a few drinks in her, she had no sense with money. She'd left her bag once at the Sphinx, and again at the homo hangout, Carroll's. She'd been lucky Shell had noticed and gone back to retrieve it before some light-fingered citizen got his hands on it. No, she never would have been able to prove Shell had taken it.

So why hadn't he? It was possible for him to live a year or more on what Sissy had been carrying around. Admittedly, Sissy was unique. He'd never met, in his years of steering tourists in Paris, anyone quite like her. Anyone so quickly compassionate at another's woes.

But the real question was, would he have taken it had it been anyone except Sissy? And if not, why not?

A matter of conscience? Don't be funny. Where do you start and where do you stop?

You start by being a free loader, a guy who goes to all the parties but never gives one, a guy who fails to ever pick up the check. Finally, you make deals for taking your supposed friends to places that will kick back to you.

You even stoop, at times, to being a gigolo, although you don't call it that, and neither does the tourist woman. But what it amounts to is sleeping with a woman who, ordinarily, you'd think too old or unattractive, a woman who picks up the check when you take her out.

What was the next step? Pimping?

He crossed the Rue de Rivoli and entered the Tuileries. To his right was the Jeu de Paume museum with its treasury of impressionist paintings from Corot to Van Gogh and Gauguin. Ordinarily, he might have stopped off, but he wasn't up to it today. He wasn't up to looking at the work of men who'd really had it.

Pimping? Why kid himself? From time to time some of the male tourists he ran into would furtively ask his advice about picking up a professional. Invariably, Shell gave good advice, even though the man was most often married. Occasionally, the girls offered him a cut. Wasn't that pimping? Just because he didn't stand on a corner whispering to passing men didn't mean he wasn't pimping.

And what came next, when you'd gone this far? Tout, gigolo, pimp. What was preventing that final step, out-and-out thief?

He emerged from the gardens onto the Quai des Tuileries and turned left, passing the endless bookstalls along the quayside with their mélange of second-hand books, old prints, decorative maps—and pornography. Some of the stall owners nodded or called to him.

Shell got a fifty per cent kickback from these peddlers of filth in print. It could mount up. A smirking, half-ashamed American tourist would spend fantastic amounts for the privilege of reading four-letter words, or looking at completely nude photographs. The French had some strange ideas pertaining to dirty books. They were strict about such material written in *French*, but couldn't care less what you published in English or some other foreign language.

Shell grunted his self-contempt. Where had it all started? He let his mind go back …

* * * *

It had probably started before his birth, with Marian Gelbert and George Halliday. Marian Gelbert had edited the college yearbook, had starred in the senior class production of *As You Like It* and was president of the Thespian Society and the Glee Club. Marian Gelbert, of whom they had said so many flattering things in the graduation book. Hollywood? New York? London? Paris? Where was the talented Marian Gelbert going to go after graduation?

She didn't go anywhere.

She stayed in New Elba, Ohio, and married George Halliday who never quite got over his good luck. It was always a source of amazement to the plodding George that as pretty and gifted a girl as Marian could ever have chosen him when all the world should have been beating a path to her door.

He had never admitted the drawbacks of being married to her. He had never complained when, upon returning home, tired from a twelve-hour day at his hardware supplies emporium, he was confronted with the fact that the evening was to be spent listening to Marian giving readings to the Shakespeare Club. When informed that his garage was to be converted into a workshop for the Handicrafts Association, complete with pottery wheels and looms, he had merely nodded acquiescence.

Nor had he interfered with her grandiose plans upon the birth of Shelley. Secretly, he would have liked to name the boy Charles or James, feeling that an offbeat nickname was a handicap in the world of small boys. But Shelley it was and, during the months when she had been carrying the baby, Marian made a point of reading aloud the poetry of the British Romantic Period at least two hours a day on the off chance that there might be something to the theory that you could influence an unborn child. For nine months it had been Shelley, Keats and Byron and a multitude of lesser lights such as Leigh Hunt and Thomas Moore. George Halliday had got poetry thrown at him until he finally knew long stanzas by heart without having made the least effort to recall them.

And, secretly, he was relieved that by the time the boy was old enough to read, Marian had switched her ambitions toward art. Painting was far enough out, he figured, but at least it wasn't as bad as having a poet in the family.

Marian Halliday took her task seriously. Little Shelley learned to sketch before he learned to write. Crayons became his toy, in spite of any desires he might have had in other directions. He had water colors and even oils with which to daub at an age when other kids were brandishing cap pistols.

Four years of art in high school—and, of course, he led the class. Miss Thompson, the art teacher, admitted that Shelley Halliday was the most talented lad she had ever taught. A Leonardo da Vinci in embryo, she'd said.

Four more years of art at Antioch, and although his instructors there had not quite the same ecstatic opinions of his abilities that had Miss Thompson, that could, at least partly, be laid to professional pique. As his mother pointed out, art, after you have gone beyond the elementary principles, can hardly be taught. Each artist can only paint in his own style and each new developing creator of beauty on canvas must find his own milieu.

College over, Shelley Halliday had spent some eight months getting together enough canvases to hold a one-man show in a Cincinnati gallery. It was a triumph. The expense of the opening, at which Marian Halliday insisted champagne be served in abundance and the hors d'oeuvres catered by the swankest restaurant in town, set George Halliday back plenty but the paintings sold beyond expectation. After all expenses, and the forty per cent commission deducted by the gallery owner, Shell even had a slight profit. Most of the sales, admittedly, went to relatives and friends, although two were taken by the New Elba High School to be displayed in the foyer. Before the show was over, half his offerings had been purchased, and Shell Halliday had some excellent art reviews to go into his scrapbook. The Cincinnati papers had been more than kind.

Marian Halliday began her campaign to send Shell to Paris for a year of extended study. At first she had dreams of accompanying him, but there George Halliday put his foot down. His business was moderately prosperous but it most certainly wasn't up to supporting two people in Paris. Besides, Marian Halliday might be in her forties now but she was still the most beautifully desirable thing that had ever happened in the life of George Halliday and he wasn't about to give her up.

The boy? Well, they'd find some way of giving him his year of extensive study in Paris, but he'd be on his own.

They had planned it in detail one night in the parlor, the four of them, Marian, George, Shell and Connie. And it was decided that the only thing which made sense was for Shell to keep going. The prospect of entering into George Halliday's business after all these years of study was ridiculous. This was no time to hesitate. Marian explained that that had been her own mistake—although at this point she cast a loving glance at her stolid husband—because she, too, had been talented and who knew how far she might have gone had she stuck it out and gone to Hollywood or New York?

Yes, Connie had been present, too. Constance Lockwood, the childhood sweetheart, the girl who lived three doors down the street. Connie Lockwood, blond of hair, long of leg. A trifle on the plumpish side, in her early twenties, but on Connie and at this age, it wasn't amiss. A somewhat plumpish version of Debbie Reynolds, Shell had thought.

Even Connie had agreed, since even she had the dream. A painter, a real painter who had studied in Paris. One day, Shell would be the greatest painter in the Middle West. Who knew? Perhaps in all America. When you looked at the tripe the others were selling for fabulous prices, how could Shell miss?

After the family conference, Shell and Connie had driven off in the four-year-old Buick of George's and had continued the discussion from their own viewpoint.

They sat in the back seat and there was preliminary necking which had become so patterned over the years they'd gone steady together as to be almost routine.

And then they'd talked a bit further—about whether or not they should have dates with others during the year of separation. And they'd both been noble and decided to be modern and not ridiculous and of course they'd have other dates. But once again, of course, it wouldn't be allowed to become serious.

In spite of the fact that the night was moonless there was sufficient light to give Connie's blond beauty an all but ethereal quality. Shell felt a stirring within him that he'd learned to suppress when alone with her.

It wasn't that he was completely inexperienced with women. Not after four years away at school. He'd had short affairs and he'd had a few experiences with the pros and semi-pros that abound in the vicinity of a campus. But Connie was for keeps, and you didn't soil your own nest.

But now?

He kissed her again and fondled one youthful breast in his hand. That much was permissible. They'd worked it out years ago—just what was allowed and what wasn't. Never in words, but there was an unspoken rule.

She wore a sweater. While he pressed home his kiss, forcing her lips gently apart with his tongue, he pulled the sweater free from her skirt and slipped his hand beneath. This was dangerously near the forbidden point, but she stirred without protest.

At twenty-two, Connie Lockwood needed a brassiere only for purposes of modesty, not support. Tonight, she wore none. Her breast was warm and responsive to his fingers. And now he was past the line of permission.

There seemed to be an explosion. Something happened to time. There was an interval which Shell Halliday could never remember afterward, which he would have given a great deal to have remembered in later months of loneliness.

Connie's skirt was now up to her thighs, gathered into her lap. Her long legs gleamed shockingly white in the little light provided him.

He was stroking the pinkness of her inner thighs, muttering into her open, hot mouth, and he could feel himself throbbing with need.

She moaned and evidently heard the sound of belt buckle and zipper, because she suddenly sat more upright and drew in her breath in fear. But still her skirt remained drawn up in her lap, and still her legs gleamed white.

When she spoke, her voice was remarkably even considering the pressure they'd both allowed themselves to build up.

"Darling," she said, avoiding looking at him, avoiding seeing what was there. "Darling, if you must do this, all right. I can't deny you tonight. I know it's partly my fault but—you stir me as much as I do you."

He muttered something incomprehensible and pressed closer to her. His maleness was obvious.

She said, her voice dogged, "But, darling, if you do, I think … perhaps … you'll be sorry forever. Something will have gone out of our love if you take me now."

He tried to bring his thoughts back to reality.

"Look, Connie, that's ridiculous. We've been practically engaged since you were a freshman in high school. Nothing can end it now. And … I'm going away."

"I know," she said simply. "If you feel you must, then you may. But … darling …"

"You don't want to, do you?" he said bluntly.

"Darling, I would rather our … first time not be in the back of a car, like a pair of furtive adolescents."

"We could go to a motel."

She said, very softly, "Then it would be less adolescent, perhaps, but I feel I would still be—*we* would still be—degrading ourselves. And, Shell, after all these years, I would like to have the white I wear as a bride mean what it's supposed to mean. A symbol of—don't laugh at me—purity."

The peak of his passion had ebbed away. He realized she was being slightly corny and dramatic, but …

Shell Halliday adjusted his clothes. "Okay, honey. You win."

She buried her head in her hands for a moment. "I'm … I'm not sure I'm glad that I did," she said. He helped her smooth her skirt down.

* * * *

He was crossing the Seine on the Pont du Carrousel.

Yes, Connie. That had been a great part of it. He couldn't go back and face Connie. It would have been bad enough with his mother. George Halliday would have been fine. He probably would have preferred that Shell live in New Elba and work in the store, finally to inherit it. Yes, that would have been his father's position.

But his mother? And especially Connie?

When he had arrived in Paris, he spent the first week in looking about and in investigating the various masters who taught advanced art. There had been four or five at that time whom Shell considered worth working under.

It had taken a week to get located. The master under whom he wanted to study and a small studio apartment in which to live. All very Parisian and in the tradition of young foreign art students come to the City of Light to pursue their work at the font of the world's art center.

It had taken him a week to get located and a month to find out he was no artist. He'd already made the discovery before the French master had apologetically taken him aside and told Shelley Halliday that he could no longer take his money. His conscience wouldn't allow it.

There had been another teacher for a time, one whose conscience wasn't quite so strong, but Shell had been kidding himself. He was pouring money down a drain. He knew enough about art to know good work and talent when he saw it, and he wasn't seeing it on his own canvas.

In fact, he even wondered how he'd been able to delude himself back in Ohio.

So it took him a month to find out he was no artist, and never would be, and it took him the rest of the year to figure out how he was going to explain the fact back home. How was he going to spend the rest of his life walking the streets of New Elba, listening to the whispers?

There goes Shell Halliday. Used to set himself up as an artist—even went to Paris. Wasted thousands of dollars of old George Halliday's money. Can't draw a line. Had to come crawling home and take a job in his father's store.

He continued to walk down Rue des Saints-Pères and turned left on Saint Germain. He passed the Deux Magots where he'd provoked the meeting with Sissy and Mike Brett-James the evening before and considered, momentarily, having an *apéritif.* But no, he still had the remnants of a hangover. He walked on toward his hotel and continued his thoughts.

He had never figured out how to break the news to family and friends. He cut out his studies and slipped into Left Bank expatriate society. Students, drunks, would-be artists, models, pretty and otherwise, homosexuals, nymphomaniacs, poets, writers, sculptors, musicians, refugees, titled and otherwise, and just plain, garden-variety international bums.

It was easy enough, particularly that first year when he still had his father's money, and the little studio apartment soon became a hangout for the set he moved in.

Aside from sketching vicious little caricatures of the people of the Latin Quarter, both resident and tourist, he forgot about work at all. It was easy to do, particularly while the money lasted.

He wrote dutifully to his parents and to Connie and, at first, his letters were moderately honest. He avoided mentioning his supposed studies. But that wouldn't do, they wanted details of his life. So he began stretching a point here and there, mentioning name artists he met and associated with, pretending to discuss the painting he was currently working upon, dropping a hint that he was progressing continually.

And, finally, he got to the point where he mentioned participating in a show at this gallery or that. Occasionally he'd mention selling a painting.

At the end of the year, he came up with his answer. He wasn't going home. At the time he was living with a Polish model, a dark, excitable girl still in her late teens. She was a volcano in bed.

He wrote George Halliday, explaining that he'd have to continue his studies, that a year wasn't long enough, that he still had a lot to learn. The letter hadn't been easy to write. It helped that he'd just come off a three-day binge and sexual spree with the Polish girl. A splitting headache can go far toward stilling a conscience.

To Shell's shock, George Halliday wrote back that further support was impossible. The current recession had hit town and the Halliday store was feeling the fall in employment. He could send a few hundred dollars, enough to bring Shell home, but that was all. Shell would have to return and start selling his paintings, or open a gallery or art school, or whatever it was that artists did to make a living. George Halliday was sorry, and Marian greatly upset, but financial facts were facts and they just couldn't afford to keep Shell abroad.

There was a check for four hundred dollars. Shell cashed it and went back to the model and another binge.

When his rent was up, he moved from his studio to a single room in a Left Bank hotel. And a few weeks later he moved from there to a cheaper hotel and began investigating the facts of life as they pertain to those on a shoestring budget in Paris.

There were various angles. For instance, you could get the gasoline coupons that were issued to the foreigner by the government. They gave a considerable discount from the usual dollar a gallon price, and they could be sold easily on the black market. It was far from a living but it helped out each month. And he signed up as a student at the Sorbonne and got a student pass which enabled him to get discounts on the metro and other transportation, gave him free or cheap entry to much entertainment, and allowed him to eat at government-subsidized student restaurants for a pittance.

And he began free loading on those who had formerly free-loaded on him, although that didn't last long. The Left Bank crowd in which he moved were past masters in avoiding a touch.

Early in the game he discovered that for the usual tourist, especially Americans, there was an aura around the Bohemian, the Latin Quarter poet, painter, or whatever. Prosperous businessmen and their wives from Far Cry, Nebraska were hot to meet a "real Bohemian" and willing, even anxious, to pick up the tab for the privilege.

So Shell had bought a beret to wear, and made a practice of donning his most aged and paint-bespattered clothing, taking a sketch pad and hanging about the internationally known sidewalk cafés. At first it had merely been a matter of free meals and drinks, but in no time at all he found he could parlay that up to getting kickbacks from less popular restaurants and night spots to which he'd steer his wide-eyed tourists.

And still he wrote home his letters of success, describing the parties he attended—or gave—describing the internationally famous with whom he supposedly associated.

Shell had now reached Monsieur Le Prince, turned up it and then right again on Rue Casimir DeLavigne. He was just around the corner from Robert's and probably could have gone in and buttered up the headwaiter into a free lunch, but he didn't feel hungry.

Shell Halliday entered the Lycée Hotel and approached the tiny reception desk. Cyril Hobbs came out of the private apartment he and his shrill wife maintained on the ground floor.

"Any mail?" Shell asked, yawning.

"A cable and two letters," Hobbs said. He was a wizened old man, a Barry Fitzgerald type. Story had it that he was a deserter from the British army in World War I and had never returned to England. His French wife supposedly put up the money for the lease on this old fleabag.

Hobbs had the cable and letters in his hand, but he held them for a moment as he said flatly, "It's the third of the month."

"Oh?" Shell said, registering surprise. He dug his hand into a pocket and brought forth some of his take of the night before. "I'll let you have enough for two weeks, on account."

"When we gave you that room at a discount," Hobbs said wearily, "it was with the understanding that you would pay by the month and strictly on time."

Shell began to explain something about money coming through from the sale of a painting but Hobbs handed him the letters and waved a hand negatively. "All right, all right," he said.

Shell started up the stairs, ripping open the cable as he went. It was from Bigelow Warren and it read: ARRIVING ON THIRD SEE ME AT GEORGE FIFTH SOONEST.

The third? That was today. Bigelow Warren! Well, happy days were here again. Shell wouldn't have to worry about food, liquor and a bit of spending money for the next couple of weeks, at least. The cartoonist was undoubtedly in town for one of his periodic binges.

One of the letters was from Connie Lockwood. He scanned it quickly. Happy days were no longer here again.

CHAPTER 3

THE RELEVANT part of Connie's letter was in the first paragraph.

> *Darling, darling! Surprise, surprise! I'm coming to Paris! It's been so long, so very long, and I just can't wait another year, nor even a month. I'm afraid with all your prominent friends, with all those beautiful French girls (yes, darling, I'm jealous), with all the wonderful distractions which you write about, that you'll forget your poor little New Elba me. At any rate, I'm coming.*

There was more. She'd received a small inheritance from some uncle Shell had never even heard about. It was enough for the trip. She asked various questions. How should she come, by ship or air? What kind of clothing should she bring? There was a lot of the romantic gushing that was typical of small-town Connie Lockwood. But the important part was all there in the first paragraph.

His thoughts took off both ways from the middle. Not only was she coming—and he had no illusions about being able to turn her back—but evidently she could hardly wait. It might take her a week or so to get a passport, but then she'd be on her way.

He climbed the five floors to the tiny upper room that was his and pushed open the door. He seldom bothered to lock it. There wasn't anything worth stealing. Even had there been, no sneak thief would have bothered to climb this far in this cheap a hotel. Property is safe when you have insufficient to worry about.

He sat on the side of the sagging bed, faintly surprised to find it properly made. The aged maid often didn't go to the trouble of doing the rooms on the top floor. They were all taken by such as Shell Halliday; students, expatriates on their uppers, unsuccessful artists. And most of them were usually in arrears with their rent.

His eyes went around the room: The small table, the two rickety chairs, his easel—long untouched—and his palette and paints, gathering dust. Against the wall were a dozen or so of his paintings, mostly unfinished. A washbowl, a bidet, two suitcases stuck under the bed, a warped, plywood wardrobe, and a cheap Van Gogh print stuck on the wall with a pin. That was it.

He tried to picture Connie here, her eyes going around the walls, the furniture, the drabness, even the dirt. The Lockwoods were only moderately well off, even by New Elba standards, but he doubted if Connie had ever, in her some twenty-five years of life, seen anything like this except in a movie.

He tried to picture Connie and wasn't sure that he could. Four years, five years—exactly how long was it? He tried to bring her to mind, and although he could do a fairly good job on her figure, her clothing, the way she walked, ridiculously, every time he tried to recall her face it was Sissy Patterson's that intruded on his mental eye.

Connie. How did he *really, truly* feel about Connie now? Why … why … he loved her, of course. It had always been Connie, almost as far back as he could remember. Yes, of course he loved her. And someday, somehow, all the old dreams would come about—someway. And it would be Connie and Shell, just as they'd always planned.

Damn it. He felt confused and, for some reason, angry.

Shell put down the letter and looked at the cable again. Bigelow Warren was arriving in town today.

Of all the celebrities Shell had written home about, Bigelow was the only one he really knew. Bigelow Warren, the Mort Sahl of the cartoon strip. Bigelow Warren, the new darling of the world of satire, with his little-boy character, *Bobby*, who made such biting comments on the adult world of politics, socio-economics, world affairs and even religion. No sacred cow was safe from the barbs of little *Bobby*, who provoked the most sophisti-cated to gales of belly-laughter—to the great profit of his originator.

Shell had met the humorist under circumstances typical of the two of them. Bigelow, dead drunk and open to the exploitation of anyone from B-girl to cutthroat, of which there are ample of both in the world of Paris night life. Shell, looking for a mark, some tourist to whom to show the sights.

Somehow, it hadn't worked out as usual. A spark seemed to strike them both and their strange friendship began. Shell Halliday saw the cartoonist back to his Right Bank hotel, got him to bed and left, without realizing a cent.

To his surprise, he met the fellow again the following night, once again stoned to the gills and in a Montparnasse clip joint where your chances of not being taken for everything you carried in your wallet were negligible. Bigelow recognized him and fell on his neck. Nothing would do but they must see the town together, Bigelow Warren picking up the tabs, and Shell seeing he wasn't clipped.

Shell had him back to his hotel by two in the morning.

And the following night, he ran into him still again.

This time they made a business deal. Bigelow explained, owlishly, that he was on a *wee vacation* and while about it had decided to see if he could make the French vintners put on an extra shift. If Shell would act as his companion, remaining moderately sober himself so that he could keep an eye on Warren, he'd pick up all the checks and pay ten dollars a night to boot.

That had been more than three years ago and, ever since, Bigelow Warren turned up two or three times a year for one of his two-week to a month blowouts. He was a periodic drunk who didn't touch the stuff back in New York, saving it for the big binge the need for which sooner or later welled up from within. His inner bitterness didn't all distill in the acrid words with which *Bobby* castigated society.

* * * *

Shell made a decision. Face it, after more than four years in Paris, Bigelow was the nearest thing to a friend he had. He'd see what the humorist had to say.

He stripped out of his corduroys, tossed them over a chair negligently and brought his tweed suit from the closet. He got his last clean shirt from a suitcase, selected a tie and made himself presentable enough to enter the swank halls of the George Fifth Hotel, that home of the celebrity-seeking, restless American abroad.

The George Fifth was on the avenue of the same name and right down from the Champs Elysées. In spite of the expense, Shell didn't feel like further exercise today. He'd had too little sleep, too much drink and horizonal refreshments the night before and, besides, his thoughts were still playing anguished hopscotch. He took a cab.

The George Fifth is the old standby of the Hollywood, Broadway, Miami Beach crowd seeking their own kind, bright lights, a *real* dry martini and whatever else it is that café society seeks. It was only midafternoon but Shell knew the bar, which was through the lobby and shortly down the hall to the right, would be packed. He hesitated momentarily, wanting a drink now, then remembered the prices and made straight for the desk to get Bigelow's suite number. There'd be a drink there. There was always a drink in the vicinity of Bigelow Warren when he came to Paris.

The cartoonist, admittedly, wasn't afraid to spend his money. He'd confided to Shell once that he was able to deduct practically all the expense of his Paris binges from taxes. He marked his visits down to business and, for that matter, did consult some of his European markets while on the Continent. He'd spend two or three days on business and two or three weeks on his pub crawling, and evidently even Uncle Sam was satisfied.

At the George Fifth he had what must have been one of the largest suites in a hotel that trended to swank suites. By the looks of it, two or three bedrooms, as many baths, and a living room large enough to throw a good-sized dance in. As usual, on seeing such opulence, Shell closed his eyes in pain.

He said accusingly, "What are you doing with a pad this size? You won't average four hours out of the twenty-four in it."

Bigelow Warren laughed hugely, switched the glass he held in his right hand to his left and greeted Shell with warmth.

"Shell!" he crowed. "Come on in. Have a drink, man. You look like life's been getting you down. Have a brandy. Civilized drink. None of this whiskey stuff. Yep, whiskey is for hillbillies."

Shell looked him up and down and grinned wanly. Same old Bigelow Warren. A shaggy edition of Jack Carson, playing a not too comic part of a periodic drunk. Possibly six foot two and as much as two-twenty in weight. He was a bear of a man, only his good posture and continual nervous activity kept anyone from thinking of him as overweight.

When he was drinking, Shell had seen him put away a bottle of either whiskey or cognac before noon, and then, hardly started, go out on the town, not winding up until dawn.

Bigelow took in his Parisian guide, bodyguard and wassailing companion. Shell Halliday, somewhere short of thirty and already—temporarily, at least—out of life's running. Bigelow didn't know the full Halliday story, but he didn't have to. It was the same you'd hear in Hollywood, on Broadway—or in Milan, if your forte was music. The artist who didn't make it. The writer who didn't make it. The opera singer—with a frog in his throat. The defeated.

But he was still a good-looking man, Bigelow decided. A good face, a body not yet gone to pot in spite of the life Shell must lead. And, to Bigelow Warren's belief, a good heart underneath that margarine spread of cynicism.

Bigelow led him back to the side table where already was collected at least a dozen bottles, a huge silver thermos bowl of ice, a score of glasses of assorted sizes and all the other equipment for a well-turned-out bar.

His own glass was empty. As Bigelow refilled it he read off his collection. "Anything you want, Shell. Scotch, rye, bourbon, rum, vodka, cognac, Armagnac, Metaxa—"

"What the hell is Metaxa?" Shell asked.

"Metaxa, you ignorant clod, is Greek brandy. Stone-age stuff. I'm on a brandy kick. Unless I forget, I'm going to drink only brandy this vacation. Friend of mine in Philly told me you didn't have so much of a hangover on brandy. Made from grapes. Very healthy. Properly aged. No fusil oil or whatever it is you take out of whiskey by sticking it in charred oak casks for a few years."

"I'll have Scotch," Shell said. "Look, how long are you over for this time, Biggy?"

The cartoonist looked down into his glass. "I don't know. I'm all caught up on the *Bobby* strip. Besides, I've got a larger staff now. All I have to do is feed them some ideas and they do all the work. Hell, I don't even have to do that. I've got two full-time gag men—you've met Sammy and Bill. All I have to do is okay or jazz up a little, the ideas they get. Maybe I'll stay for a month this time."

Shell grunted, pouring his own whiskey and adding soda and ice. "A month. Wow. At the pace you go, no man nor beast could stand a month."

"Well, I think I'll take it easier this time." Saying which, the big man threw back his current drink and poured another.

"Ha," Shell said sourly.

Warren looked at him again, up and down. "Where'd you get that suit, Shell? Have you lowered your standards a fraction and turned to pickpocketing?"

Shell looked at him in moderate indignation. "What kind of a crack is that? I have my legitimate sources of income. Among other things, I sold a couple of paintings last week."

The cartoonist, who'd made his way back to a divan and slumped onto it, looked at Shell in surprise. "Sold two paintings? Two of *your* paintings?"

"Well, no," Shell admitted. "I met a tourist last week who wanted to buy a painting in Paris but was afraid he'd be taken by a gallery. Since I was an artist myself, he thought I could help."

"Why didn't you show him your own stuff?" Biggie wanted to know, his eyes bright with amusement.

"I did. He didn't like it."

"So?"

"So I took him to Jan Luchtvaart's studio. Jan sold him a Montmartre street scene and one of the Seine."

"And you got a cut from Jan?"

Shell shrugged defensively. "A gallery would charge Jan forty per cent for anything they sold for him. Why shouldn't I get a cut? Sure, he paid me." Shell took a chair, too, and sipped unhappily at the drink.

Bigelow was frowning. "Enough to buy that suit? It must have been quite a sale."

"Special deal," Shell admitted. "I've been lining up this tailor as somebody to take tourists to and I talked him into doing this outfit up by way of a sample I can show any prospective customers."

Bigelow got up and walked to his improvised bar and took up his bottle. He was shaking his head. "With your kind of mind, I wonder you don't go back to the States and get rich on Wall Street."

Shell looked down into his glass, empty now.

"Look, Biggy, I *can't* go back."

His drinking companion looked down on him. "Yep, I noticed something was wrong when you walked in here. What's up, Shell? Can I help?"

Shell got to his feet and poured himself another whiskey. "I doubt it," he said. "Did I ever tell you—maybe in my cups—what I'm doing in Paris?"

Bigelow narrowed his eyes slightly, thoughtfully. "Not all at once, but over a period of time I've more or less picked it up. You were the home town's pride, kind of Michelangelo come out of the Midwest, so everybody saw you off at the train, that sort of thing. And then you found out when you got over here that you didn't have it on the ball."

"That's about it, actually," Shell growled.

"And you couldn't face going home."

Shell handed him Connie's letter. "This came today," he said simply.

Warren squinted into his face a moment, then down at the letter. He read the first few paragraphs but didn't bother to finish it. He said, "The girl back home, eh?"

"Yeah."

"You've been writing them you're a big success over here."

"That's right."

"Hasn't anybody from the home town ever come over before, in all these years?"

"Once or twice. New Elba isn't very big. And then I pretended to be out of the city when they showed up. But I can't do that this time."

Bigelow looked at the first paragraph of the letter again and raked a beefy hand back through his perpetually ruffled hair. "No, I guess not. She's on her way, all right, and you're not going to be able to chill it."

They sat for a moment, drinks forgotten, and Shell stared morosely at the floor.

Bigelow growled, "You could write her and say you're married to an Italian countess or something."

"No. No, I couldn't do that."

"Still go for her, eh?"

Shell twisted his face, unaccountably disturbed by the question. "Well, all the way back to high school it's always been Connie."

"I see."

Bigelow got up, went to the sideboard and brought back the bottle of Scotch. He poured a stiff slug into Shell's glass, then poured himself one, forgetting his oath to drink only cognac.

"You could go back and face the music," Biggie suggested. "Isn't there any kind of work you could do back home to make a living for her?"

"Theoretically, I could go into my father's hardware business."

"Theoretically?"

Shell shifted his shoulders bitterly. He held up two fingers and brought them together. "Look, for four years I've been telling them Picasso and I are like this."

They thought about it some more. "Damn it," Bigelow said, "I came over here to drown my own sorrows, not to worry about somebody else's."

"What've *you* got in the way of sorrows?" Shell grunted. His eyes were on the floor again.

Bigelow shot a glance at him and for a moment his usually open face was bleak. But he said, softly, "Yeah." Then, "Well, let's see. I'm supposed to be an idea man. Or used to be before I started hiring my ideas."

His expression lit up. "Listen."

Shell looked up at him.

The heavy-set cartoonist began pacing the floor, nervously. "Listen. I got it. Yep, I think I've got it."

He hurried down to the end of the room, hurried back. He pounded one fist into the other a couple of times as though impatiently waiting a final point or two to be cleared.

"Now listen," he said finally. "You'll let her come."

Shell said bitterly, "How could I stop her, short of writing I'd just contracted leprosy?"

"No, listen. You let her come and when she arrives, you'll play the part you've been writing them about all these years. You'll be the big successful Paris artist."

"Ha," Shell snorted.

"No, wait. You'll move in here. Except for the Ritz, it's probably the only hotel in Paris she's ever heard of. Swankiest place in town."

Shell was staring again.

Bigelow was carried away. He stopped pacing and pointed his finger at Shell. "You'll move in here with me, but we'll tell it the other way. We'll pretend I'm a guest of yours. Does she know who I am? Do they run the *Bobby* strip in your home-town paper?"

"We read the Cincinnati papers. They run it there. She knows who you are, all right."

"Fine. I can be one of your celebrity friends."

"We'd never get away with it."

"Sure we would. You haven't heard all of it. We'll round up a bunch of the Left Bank crowd—artists, poets, a few of those titled refugees who haven't got a pot to plant a flower in but do have real titles, real manners and accents. We'll throw a party to end all parties. I doubt if this Connie girl friend of yours knows the names of any French artists except, perhaps, Picasso and we can tell her he's out of town. We'll fake a telegram saying he's sorry he can't come and meet your girl."

As the idea grew with the telling, Bigelow Warren became more and more happy with it.

"Yeah, fine," Shell resisted. "But sooner or later it comes to an end. You might think it was fun for a while, but you're not going to carry my load for the rest of all eternity."

"No, this is our out. After the big party, you'll get a telegram. From, say, the government Senegal, down in Dakar. They're opening up a new a stration building and want you to do a tremendous mural for them. You can't afford to miss the honor and prestige, so you sadly tell Connie you can't possibly take her to such a dangerous place as Africa and send her packing home."

"Good grief," Shell said. "She'd have the time of her life, wouldn't she?"

Bigelow tossed up his hands as though it were all solved. "Sure, she would," he agreed. "And then you could break it all off later, someway or other. You'd be over this temporary emergency, at least."

Shell said, licking his lower lip nervously, "I'd have to cable her immediately, giving this address."

"Yep. And I'll inform the desk about the change in name. I'll tell them I want to register under the pseudonym Shelley Halliday, so I won't be bothered by newspaper reporters and celebrity hunters."

"Biggy, I think it might work," Shell said, enthusiastic at last.

"Sure it'd work. It's a cinch."

Shell was suddenly deflated. "But I can't ask you to do anything like this. It'd louse up your whole trip."

"Look who's beginning to develop a conscience after all these years," Bigelow laughed.

Shell flushed.

The big man put a hand on his shoulder. "Take it easy, fella. I came over here to have a good time. Fine. This comes under that heading as far as I'm concerned. You living in this suite with me isn't going to cramp my style. In fact, I was considering asking you to move in for the duration of my stay, anyway. Much easier for you to keep your eye on me when I get stoned."

Shell stood up and took his turn at the pacing. "It'd probably work," he said.

"That's what I tell you," Bigelow said plaintively. "Now go send your cable to her. We'll do some serious drinking until she arrives."

"You know, Biggy," Shell said slowly, "you aren't the worst bastard in the world."

"That's what I keep telling people," Bigelow laughed. "But nobody believes me. Now go get your cable off. You don't want her coming to the wrong address."

Shell walked toward the door and then turned back. He said, "How come you never got married, Biggy? You've got everything to give a woman."

The other's laugh didn't quite come off. He said, "Once I was going with a girl and one night I said to her, 'Kate, let's get married,' and she said, 'It's a great idea, Biggy, but who'd have either of us?'"

"Very funny," Shell said.

* * * *

After the other had gone, Bigelow Warren looked sourly at the door. How come he'd never married? That was a good question.

He went back to the bar and took up the bottle of Scotch. No, damn it, he was going to stick to brandy, French cognac. He took up a bottle of Courvoisier and stared at the label. V.S.O.P. Twenty years old. Okay, we'll see if this winds up with a hangover.

How come he'd never got married? That was a laugh.

He opened the bottle, tossed the cork into a corner, selected a snifter glass and made his way back to the divan.

He poured a couple ounces and, instead of savoring the bouquet or flavor, tossed it back over his palate. The blood, sweat and tears of the French vintners who had produced the elegant beverage was not being appreciated at the moment. Biggy was only interested in the dulling effect their product would produce.

Shell had probably thought he was joking, but Bigelow Warren hadn't been. Who'd have him as a husband? Certainly no woman with normal desires and needs. Sure, he could find a thousand bitches who'd marry him for the money *Bobby* brought in, stay with him for a year or so, and then retire on the alimony. And there'd be no doubt about that. Any court in the land would grant a divorce to the wife of Bigelow Warren. Incompatibility.

He poured another slug of the cognac.

That Shell Halliday boy was in a bad way. Shell was a better man than he himself realized. He was becoming increasingly cynical about the hand-to-mouth ways he'd worked out to keep himself going but, fundamentally, Shell's instincts were good. He was simply going through an agonizing period of his life, caught up in a situation not actually of his own making. He'd get through it, one way or another, Bigelow was sure. Given good instinct, you got over the rough stretches, somehow.

He knocked the brandy back and poured still another. He was really beginning to feel the day's drinks by now.

What was it Shell had said? How come he, Bigelow, had never married? He had everything to give a woman.

Bigelow grunted. He had *nothing* to give a woman. That was the point.

He wished he had some cashew nuts. For some reason, he felt like sitting here, drinking Napoleon brandy and nibbling cashew nuts until the fog rolled in.

Why hadn't he ever married? He bet some of his friends figured he was as queer as a three-dollar bill.

The snifter glass was empty. He hadn't remembered drinking the last slug he'd poured. He decided, owlishly, that there was no use just sitting here and pouring a short snort at a time. He filled the big glass nearly to the brim.

When had it first happened? He could remember perfectly well, as clearly as though it had been last week instead of when he'd been a high school boy of fifteen or sixteen. Fifteen, not sixteen …

Laurie must have been at least a couple of years older, and a millennium older when it came to know-how. Up until then, Bigelow's experience had been limited to frantic necking and to wrestling with girls of his own age for the privilege of a hastily squeezed budding breast, or a hot moist hand run up under a disarranged dress to the pantieline. But Laurie? Laurie must have lost that thing most women prize when she was no older than twelve or thirteen, and Laurie had never missed it.

The only reason she'd come out with him at all was that, even at fifteen, Bigelow had the use of the family sedan and a comfortable allowance from his sales executive father. She'd been scornful of his age, but Bigelow had persisted. His contemporaries had plenty to say about Laurie, and he wanted to give it a try.

Yes, how easily it came back to him now.

After the movie, they sat in the back of the car, parked down in the Lake Hill district, far into the shade of the trees.

He'd never been with a girl who didn't protest every step he took, every kiss granted, and he was surprised when Laurie made no protest over his fumblings. Laurie was different. If anything, *she* was the aggressor, and he was nonplused.

She didn't mind having her blouse unbuttoned and then actually removed. His hands were moist as he fingered her hard-tipped breasts. He'd heard the more experienced say that the thing to do was play with a girl's breasts a little. Made her want it.

She stirred impatiently, her tongue darting into his mouth. He'd never had a girl do that before. But he'd heard about it. A soul kiss. He drew back a moment. He didn't know if he liked it or not. Kind of sloppy. At fifteen, Bigelow Warren was only a year removed from that period when he had sneered at association with girls.

"What's the matter?" she said impatiently.

"Nothing." He fumbled with her breasts some more.

"Well…?" she said.

He didn't know what was the matter with her, but her obvious impatience made him nervous.

He ran his hand up her skirt, expecting the usual playful objections, and planned on being more firm than he would have with Rachel or, say, Diana Perry.

There was no need for being firm, for wrestling or coaxing. And, to his shock, Laurie wore nothing beneath the skirt, nothing whatsoever.

That stopped him for a moment. He'd been planning his campaign, figuring on how to get her panties off, and here she wore none.

She said, all but bitterly now, "What're you waiting for?"

"Eh?" he said.

"We can't take all night."

He swallowed. "Okay," he said, tentatively and timidly lifting her skirt.

"Here," she said, and her voice was dripping with scorn now.

He hated himself for being so obviously inadequate. He imagined all the other guys must know exactly what to do under these circumstances. But, doggonnit, you had to start sometime.

She began fiddling with his clothes. That came as another shock. Always with Rachel, Rita and the others he'd been the aggressor, they the defenders of the fortress. But Laurie reached and found him wanting. She relaxed suddenly and slumped back, saying bitterly, "I should've known better."

"What's the matter, Laurie?" His voice was shaky.

"Oh, shut up," she said. "I shoulda known better than to rob the cradle."

His throat closed up. "What's the matter?" he asked hoarsely.

"Oh, go on home, little boy," she snapped. "And don't come around grown people till you learn how to follow through."

A chill went through his body.

That's as far as memory went. Bigelow Warren didn't remember the trip home. He couldn't remember if he'd driven her home or if she'd walked, or what. All he remembered was his shame and disgrace.

That was the end of that memory of inadequacy, but there were others.

His second chance had been with a divorcee of possibly thirty years, a woman with four children, aged from three to ten. And it had taken place when Bigelow was seventeen and already large for his age.

She'd been a little wisp of a woman, and very nervous about what they were doing. The encounter took place in her small home, and she was terrified that one of the children might come in. She was also afraid of possible pregnancy and insisted that he go to the drugstore for equipment.

By the time he returned, he had lost the passion they'd built up necking in the front room. However, she took him to her bedroom and there began stripping, still murmuring unhappily about the children. Without clothing, and particularly without brassiere and girdle, she was suddenly metamorphosed into a physical *something* entirely outside of Bigelow's experience.

Four children and undisciplined eating habits hadn't done her body a great deal of good.

Bigelow's experience with the female form had been confined to the photographs and pin-up girls in such magazines as *Esquire*, to statues in the museums, to girls in one-piece bathing suits on the beach. He'd never seen a fully matured woman nude before.

Something went out of him. He just *couldn't*.

She had been kind enough about it. She was mature enough to understand. Possibly she'd had failures before. Bigelow had stumbled from the house, his face flaming with embarrassment.

The next chance? Had that been the time he was with Rita? At any rate, that, too, was a failure. As soon as the girl was convinced and ready for his advance, he'd thought about his two previous failures and a cold sweat broke out on him. He became completely inadequate. The two of them covered it over, pretending they hadn't planned completion at all. They necked a little more, desultorily now, and then he took her home.

And that night he had lain in bed, staring at the ceiling and feeling the chill of inadequacy go through him. It was then he realized that he wasn't quite a *man*, that he couldn't perform with a woman. He was—what was the term?—sterile. No, that wasn't it. He was … impotent. The way old men got, when they were about seventy, or maybe not until as old as ninety. He'd read somewhere about some old duffer who gave his wife a baby at the age of ninety. And here he was, Bigelow Warren, impotent at only eighteen.

The next memory came at the age of twenty, in the college years. The gang was celebrating something or other, probably a football victory, because Bigelow had been on the second team. At any rate, it was a celebration and they'd bought several gallons of bootleg applejack.

One thing led to another. Parades, drinking, college songs, more drinking, a mad dash to escape pursuing cops—and, finally, a visit to a brothel.

Bigelow had probably dragged his heels at that point, but he didn't remember now. All that he remembered was that he was portioned out to a frowzy, flabby bottle-blonde who had efficiently conducted him to her cubicle-sized room and just as efficiently got him into bed and performed with him that act that thus far in life had been impossible for him. She performed it not once but thrice, and Bigelow remained until morning.

Oh Lord, she had looked horrible in the morning. Disgusting, revolting, stomach-churningly repulsive, but he'd been able to function normally with her.

And that had set the pattern. Drunk and with a professional, Bigelow Warren, no matter how disgusted he might be with himself, could enjoy a woman as well as the next man. Sober and with a girl who was willing to make love with him for his own sake, his own self, and he simply could not operate. It amounted to a mental block. It had been years now since he'd even tried. The embarrassment was too acute. To get a girl into bed, stark nude, and then find himself impotent and have to apologize to her, that was more than he was willing to try again.

He realized that his problem should have been taken to a psychiatrist, but somehow he couldn't face the requirement that he explain it all—his inadequacy, his fears of impotence which only brought on the very situation he dreaded. He just couldn't have told anyone, not even a doctor.

But that was how it stood. With what he considered a decent woman, Bigelow Warren was impotent. With a professional, he was as other men. So, obviously, marriage wasn't for him. Under the surface of his sophistication, Bigelow Warren had a high regard for women and for the act of love, an almost sophomoric regard. He wouldn't dream of getting drunk and going to bed with a woman he truly loved, and he knew that it was the only possible way he could satisfy his potential wife …

The fog was beginning to roll in. Bigelow Warren closed one eye, the better to focus, and estimated the amount of cognac remaining in his bottle. One good slug. He poured it into his glass and, stiff-wristed, downed it.

Let's see. Now where was he?

He was swacked, that was for sure. And that meant he was probably in Paris. He seldom went off the wagon except when he came to Paris.

Well, if he was in Paris, where was Shell? He never got swacked in Paris without old Shell to watch over him. Wasn't safe. Not the way *he* got swacked and lost all sense of time or vicinity.

Which reminded him. How long had he been in Paris? He considered that for a moment, then got up and lurched to the sideboard. What he needed was a drink—and some cashew nuts. He had an appetite for cashew nuts and now that he thought about it, it seemed he'd had this appetite for a long time. The only bottle that was open was one of Scotch. He poured some into the snifter glass and regarded it accusingly. For some reason he couldn't remember he'd sworn off Scotch. Well, he could figure it out later.

He wondered where Shell was. Damn it, he shouldn't be going out without his companion-guide-bodyguard. But he needed some cashew nuts, didn't he? He tossed back the whiskey and made his way toward the door.

It was at this point that the fog rolled in.

CHAPTER 4

BY THE TIME Shell Halliday got back to the George Fifth after sending his cable to Connie and collecting the more presentable of his things as well as his easel and other artistic trappings from his Left Bank hotel, it was getting well on into evening. He had no difficulty getting past the desk and into Bigelow Warren's suite, although there was no answer to the phone. The management of the George Fifth was used to the cartoonist's eccentricities. A guest moving in was not untoward.

He had figured, when the phone wasn't answered, that the big man had fallen asleep after Shell left. He was taken aback when he found the other had obviously gone out.

It wasn't safe for Bigelow Warren to be on the streets when in his cups—not even the streets of Paris. He could accumulate trouble without even trying.

When Shell had first met the periodic alcoholic, it had been bad enough. Almost invariably the cartoonist would go on a several-day toot and wind up in the French equivalent of the drunk tank. French drunk tanks aren't the best, especially when foreigners are involved. It usually took the assistance of the American Consulate and a French lawyer or two before Biggy was free to leave—and start in on a new binge.

In fact, there had been some question at the time Shell had first met Bigelow whether or not the French were going to declare his passport invalid for their country. He'd been in too many drink-inspired escapades for even their tolerance.

Yes, it had been bad enough three years ago, when Bigelow Warren had first met Shell. Now it was worse. At least at that time, the comic-strip artist had tried to place some limits upon himself, knowing that if he didn't he'd wind up paying off the hard way. But now, since he'd found Shell to act as a combination guide, bodyguard, apologist and baby-sitter, Biggy had given up all restraints. On the town, and tight, he let the unruffled Shell take over responsibility, knowing the other could usually get him through the tight spots and back to the hotel and to bed when the time came.

It wasn't that Bigelow was a fighting drunk, or even a particularly objectionable one in the usual sense. He was an easygoing, friendly, rumpled bear of a man even when so staggeringly stoned that all sense of location, time or anything else had disappeared. It was just that things *happened* to him.

If there was a pickpocket within half a mile, he made a beeline for Biggy Warren. If there was a B-girl or a drunk-rolling tart anywhere in the vicinity, she zeroed in on Biggy. But that wasn't the worst.

The oversized cartoonist, even though keeping a friendly surface, had no ability to stifle his acrid-cynical viewpoints, given alcoholic lubrication. And while it was one thing for cute little *Bobby* in the comic strip to make snide comments upon politics, religion, racial questions, sex, Communism and war, it was another for a king-size drunk to do it.

It wasn't deliberate. Biggy just couldn't help himself. If he managed to get into a bar conversation with a rock-bound Fundamentalist, he'd take off with some biting comment upon the inconsistencies in the Old Testament. He'd want to know where Cain's wife came from if Adam and Eve were the first two persons on the whole Earth.

If he got into a conversation with a one hundred and one per cent American of the McCarthy school, he'd start off by stating that he thought democracy was a good idea and that we ought to give it a try in the United States one of these days. Or if he was talking with an avowed Commie, he'd innocently ask when the State was going to wither away in Russia as Marx had declared was necessary before true socialism could be established.

He was in the soup, sooner or later, and usually sooner.

Shell Halliday took in the collection of bottles on the sideboard and closed his eyes in pain. By the looks of things, Bigelow had, since morning, put away almost two bottles of hard liquor.

Shell thought desperately. If the other got into any serious trouble, something that might wind him up in the jug for a time, then the whole scheme involving Connie would be clobbered. He had to find Bigelow before the cartoonist could pull some gargantuan boner.

Shell rubbed his hand over his face in quick irritation. It was still early. Where would Biggy head? He'd just started on his binge today, so it was unlikely the man would be looking for feminine companionship as yet. That usually came after a week or more of fairly steady drinking. So he probaby couldn't be found in the Pigalle section where his favorite bar was Fred Payne's.

And it was too early in the game for him to get on a sentimental jag and want to go listen to Gordon Payant sing tear jerkers. No, he wouldn't be at Gordon's.

Shell poured himself a quick Scotch and tossed it back. Confound it, he had to think. There were some eight thousand bistros in Paris, and countless bars, *caves*, cafés, and *terrasses*. Biggy could be at any of them.

The Ritz Bar! Shell snapped his fingers. The favorite hangout of the well-heeled American in Paris. And Bigelow—but no, now that he thought about it—Bigelow Warren wasn't welcome in the Ritz any more. The last time he and Shell had gone there, Shell had left him only long enough to go to the men's room, but when he'd returned, Biggy had managed to get into a noisy scrap with two Georgians on the merits of segregation, and such supposedly closely related subjects as whether or not you'd want your sister to marry a Negro.

Shell started for the door. He'd simply have to start making the rounds. It was too early for the Crazy Horse Saloon, just down the street from the hotel. And you could rule out the queer clubs, such as Le Monocle, Madame Arthur's and Carroll's. A few drinks and Bigelow was intolerant of queers; not belligerently so, but he just didn't want to be bothered with the third sex.

Given luck, Biggy might have got no further than the George Fifth Bar downstairs. But no, Shell looked in briefly and drew a zero.

At the ornate entrance, he stopped long enough to speak to the doorman. "Nicolas, have you seen Mr. Warren?"

The tall, gaunt, liveried Russian pursed his lips. A Mischa Auer type, Shell had always cast him. "Ah, Mr. Warren. He wished to know where he could purchase some cashew nuts. Perhaps twenty minutes ago."

Shell groaned. Biggy was on one of his expeditions. He'd stick to it until he met with success—or disaster. The trouble was, he'd seek his desires in the most unlikely places. Cashew nuts? He'd probably make a round of women's hairdressers, or Turkish baths, in search of them.

"What did you tell him?" Shell demanded.

The former Cossack shrugged hugely. "That the *concierge* here at the hotel would undoubtedly be able to procure these cashew nuts for him."

"And he said?"

"He didn't seem to believe me, sir. He headed that way." The doorman pointed toward the Champs Elysées.

Shell slipped him a franc, muttered his thanks and took off. If Biggy was heading in this direction, then the whole Left Bank could probably be eliminated for the time being. The big cartoonist was probably at a sidewalk café along the fashionable main tourist stem of Paris, which stretched from the Arc de Triumphe at the Place de L'Etoile, to the Place de La Concorde just before the Tuileries gardens.

Given luck, the other would settle down soon for a drink, then he'd amble along, enquiring of flower shops or jewelry stores for his cashew nuts, until the next sidewalk café.

However, it didn't work out that way. Bigelow wasn't at Fouquet's on the corner of Geroge Fifth and the Champs Elysées, at Le Deauville a hundred yards down the boulevard, nor at the Pam Pam, another fifty feet along. Shell doubted the big man would come further without a drink.

He snapped his fingers. Harry's New York Bar wasn't too far from here, at 5 Rue Daunou, near the Opéra.

* * * *

Harry's New York Bar could happen only in New York—or Paris. Fifty years ago, before the dry era in the States, it had been established on the working theory that since there was every other type of bar and restaurant in the world in Paris, there should be a New York saloon. The bar itself was imported from famous old Clancey's when that Manhattan establishment closed its doors in anticipation of Prohibition.

Complete with swinging doors, dark mahogany paneling and dim lighting, as well as hot dogs for sale at the bar, there is no question of authenticity. Behind the bar an extensive collection of paper currency is pasted to the wall, and from the ceiling hangs a picturesque conglomeration consisting of a horseshoe off Man-O-War, a pair of Primo Carnera's boxing gloves and a baseball autographed by the White Sox and Giant teams.

Harry's reached its peaks during Prohibition and during the period when Harry McElhone presided. The *lost generation* made it their center; Hemingway, Scott Fitzgerald, O. O. McIntyre, Jack Dempsey and such adopted it as their home away from home.

Bigelow Warren was an enthusiastic member of the International Bar Flies, of which Harry's was Trap Number One, and invariably got out his Bar-Fly tie and the fly glued to a lump of sugar buttonhole pin, whenever embarking on a Paris binge. Shell had high hopes of locating him at "Sank-Roo-Doe-Noo" as Harry's ads in the Paris edition of the *Herald-Tribune* always read.

But he drew another blank. There were a dozen or so Americans at the regular bar, possibly the same number at the tables in the back. They'd come far to accomplish putting their foot on a brass rail and ordering one of the forty-eight varieties of American whiskey which Harry's boasted.

Shell cast his eyes around quickly. No signs of Bigelow. However, he might be down below.

In the intimate basement rooms at the foot of the erratically winding stairs, nothing but champagne had been served in the old days and it had become a fashionable after-theatre rendezvous. Now, in the Sixties, it wasn't quite so exclusive, but still a favorite, with Charlie Lewis playing a gentle piano, and various old-timers usually present to cry into their drinks in memory of the allegedly glorious past.

Bigelow wasn't here either, but others were.

Somebody was waving from the far end. "*Shell!* Shell, over here!"

It was Sissy Patterson and, yes, Mike Brett-James was with her. Neither of them looked much the worse for their debauchery, after last night's night-club crawl.

He felt an unaccountable lift at just seeing her and, briefly, he could feel again her hand stroking his head, and her voice asking—of all things—if he wanted his back scratched. He hadn't had the time, as yet, to consider all the ramifications of Sissy Paterson and the strange impact she'd made on his way of life, and he hadn't even thought in terms of ever seeing her again. Doing so gave him a warm feeling in his … well, his belly. Almost like the impact of a shot of hard liquor when you're completely bushed and need a drink badly.

As he made his way toward their table, Shell wondered uncomfortably if the girl had told her companion about Shell Halliday's means of live-lihood—if you could call it that. Inwardly, he shrugged. A bum couldn't afford a thin skin. It wouldn't be the first time someone had caught on to Shell's steering and touting, and indicated their contempt at his way of life.

Mike wove to his feet and murmured, as though embarrassed, "How are you this evening, Shell, old man? Afraid I made a bit of an ass of myself last night."

Shell grinned and shook the proffered hand. The British always seemed to want to shake hands. He said, "As I recall, when I was putting you to bed you wanted me to kiss you good night."

"Good Heavens," Sissy laughed. "Pull up a chair, Shell. We've just got around to killing the hangover."

Shell looked at her. Fresh as a daisy, as the expression went. Vivacious, healthy, full of life, and, by the looks of her, about six or eight drinks already under her belt. "Just for a minute or so," Shell said, pulling up a chair. "I'm looking for a friend."

"I'm a friend," Sissy quipped. "Wouldn't I do? What'll you have, Shell?" Her voice changed only infinitesimally as she added, "The drinks are on me."

He darted a questioning look at her, but she hadn't meant to rub things in. Sissy wasn't the type.

"Beer," Shell said. "They've got good beer here at Harry's—draught from Munich. I've got to stay sober if I'm ever going to find Biggy?"

"Biggy?" Mike said. He, too, evidently, had had half a dozen, but hadn't the capacity of the Floridian girl. His high voice was already slurring.

"Bigelow Warren," Shell said. He added, almost defensively, as though to erect himself a small barrier of prestige after tearing himself down so far in Sissy's eyes this morning, "The cartoonist. He's a friend of mine."

Mike Brett-James was blank but Sissy said, "You mean the one who does *Bobby?* Oh, good Heavens, I'd *love* to meet him. Did you see that one where the politician is giving this big speech in the United Nations and telling about how peace-loving we are and how America has never started a war and how we've never defaulted on a treaty, and then little Bobby pipes up and says he ought to tell that to the Indians?"

Shell laughed. "Yeah, I remember that one. A howl went up from the D.A.R. and the Legion and some senator or other even brought it up in Congress. Wanted Biggy investigated as a subversive."

"Well ... isn't he kind of a pinko or something?"

Shell's beer had come. He took a quick gulp before scoffing, "Bigelow? No. He isn't anything. Just down on all sorts of pomposity and humbug, particularly when it applies to politics, international affairs, that sort of thing."

Mike had finished his drink and poured another from the half empty bottle of Johnny Walker which stood on the table. He was further along than Shell had first thought. He closed one eye and looked unsteadily at Shell. "You know, my dear chap, you look considerably nicer than you did in those corduroys yesterday."

"Well, thanks," Shell said. "Those were my working clothes."

Sissy giggled and winked at him. Obviously, she hadn't discussed Shell with Mike Brett-James and just as obviously, she was still as philosophical about Shell's manner of making a living as she had been that morning when they were in bed together.

Mike waggled a finger at him. "You look ... well ... younger. And ... very good-looking."

Shell laughed. "Thanks, Mike. I'll have to wash my face and wear a clean shirt more often. You look very natty yourself."

"Good Heavens, let's all have another drink and stop throwing compliments back and forth—that is, of course, unless you want to throw them at me," Sissy said. She signaled the waiter for another mug of beer for Shell.

"Look," Shell protested, "I've got to take it easy."

"You can't get anywhere on beer," Sissy said. "Listen, Shell, now that Mike has evidently decided that you aren't trying to woo me away from him, and that you're more acceptable in tweeds than corduroys—"

"Oh now, my dear—" Mike began.

"—why don't you come along with us to dinner? We've made reservations again at Maxim's."

"Sorry," Shell said. "I really do have to find Bigelow Warren. It's very important."

She made a moue but didn't press the point.

While Shell finished his second beer, they rehashed the evening before, laughing at his highlights. Sissy insisted again that she'd never had such fun.

Shell said, finally, "Look, pardon me for a moment. I've got to visit the little boys' room. Munich beer isn't any better than any other when it comes to this problem."

Mike weaved to his feet, too. Shell was beginning to suspect that the Englishman had never fully recovered from last night's drinking and was simply hanging one on atop the last.

"I'll go, too," he insisted.

"I thought only women couldn't go to the powder room alone," Sissy commented.

"Fear not, we shall return!" Shell announced grandly.

Mike giggled as though that had been preposterously funny and wended his way after the American who headed for the men's room next to the basement's tiny auxiliary bar, and at the foot of the stairs leading up to Harry's proper.

There was no misaking the entrance to the men's room. The sign on the door read: *Gents, Messieurs, Herren, Homines, Señores, Signori* and one or two more, including the Greek. The room itself was moderately small; a toilet in a separate booth, two urinals, one lavatory before a large mirror and a monstrous red towel on the door. There was plenty of room, without crowding, for two. Shell couldn't understand the Englishman's pressing against him.

He frowned and looked back over his shoulder. "What's the matter, Mike, you sick?"

The Englishman gave a half-embarrassed chuckle, his face whitish and strange. He murmured, "Did I really ask you to kiss me good-night, dear boy?"

Shell scowled at him. "Yeah. Yeah, you did. You were as drunk as a coot. Look, you're kind of tight right now, aren't you, Mike?"

Brett-James giggled. "I wasn't as drunk as all that, dear boy. Nor am I as gullible as I may seem. I realize that you're, ah, pardon the expression, dear boy, *on the town* so to speak ..."

Shell was staring now. He couldn't quite believe the other was getting through to him correctly.

The Englishman's expression went sly and, in a way, fawning. "You obviously were making your percentage last night." He held up a hand, anticipating Shell. "Oh, not that I care a bit. What I was leading up to ... well, if you're looking for ways to make a few francs ..." He giggled foolishly again. "Well, why don't you pop up to my room tonight?"

Before he could control himself, moving automatically, Shell had lashed out backhanded across the other's face, staggering the homosexual back against the lavatory.

Immediately he was sorry. Shell Halliday wasn't the kind of pseudo he-man who insisted on proving his claims to masculinity by beating up a type of unfortunate for whom he was actually sorry. He'd never hit a queer before in his life. For that matter, he realized quickly and grimly, he probably had this insult coming to him. He was a self-made tout, a steerer, a percentage man. Possibly Brett-James had a right to suspect that Shell wasn't above other methods of picking up a quick buck.

At any rate, he was instantly ashamed. He said gruffly, irritably, "I'm sorry. I shouldn't have done that." He turned to go.

Michael Brett-James had cowered back into the corner before the mirror, both hands to his face and his eyes wide with bewilderment, hurt and fear. He took one of his hands away from his nose and looked at it. "You've broken my nose," he whined. It was bleeding.

"I doubt it," Shell growled uncomfortably. "You've just got a bloody nose. It'll go away."

"Oh … no," the other wailed. Shell wondered why he hadn't spotted the other as a homo sooner. He had a certain feminine quality about him, now that you looked for it.

"No," Mike wailed. "When I get a bloody nose, it lasts ever so long."

"Well, there's nothing I can do about it," Shell snapped. "Here, take my handkerchief. What do you expect, first aid?"

"Oh, it's all your fault," Mike wailed, "and Felicity was going to take me to Maxim's. I *love* dining at Maxim's. I just *can't* have her see me like this."

Shell said flatly, "Then go on back to your hotel. I'll tell her that you took suddenly ill of alcoholic poisoning or something."

The other looked at him obliquely. "And you won't tell her…?"

"I'll tell her anything I damn well please," Shell barked and turned and pushed his way out of the small room, irritated at the whole affair. He had troubles enough of his own without getting involved in this sort of nonsense.

* * * *

Back at the table, Shell gave a quick, inaccurate description of Mike's alleged illness and resumed his chair. Sissy seemed only moderately distressed at her escort's departure, probably too far gone herself, he decided, to care one way or the other. He couldn't figure out her relationship to the Englishman.

Actually, he know he should be out looking for Bigelow Warren, but the girl had a more than ordinary interest for him. Somehow or other she wasn't just another quick roll in the hay, of the type he enjoyed all too often in his way of life.

He said cautiously, "What's with this Mike Brett-James, Sissy?"

"How do you mean?" She'd been listening to the pianist who was softly playing the tunes of the Twenties, and running over *Me and My Shadow* at this point.

"I don't know. He seems to have a sort of proprietory air."

She shifted shapely shoulders. "He wants to marry me."

"Wants to marry you?" he blurted.

She frowned in quick irritation. "What's wrong with that?"

He turned cautious again. "Nothing, of course. You haven't known each other very long though, have you?"

"No. Not really."

"Then it's his idea, not yours?"

She looked at him for a moment as though she were going to make a tart reply to that, but then evidently changed her mind. "I think there's a rather good chance of my taking him up, Shell," she said simply.

It was none of his business. None at all, Shell told himself. Damn it, why didn't he take off and go looking for Bigelow? Everything was going to be in the soup if he didn't find the burly cartoonist before the other could get into a pot of trouble.

But he said, "Well, I mean, after last night and this morning ..." His voice was hesitant. "... well, you can't be very much in love with him."

She scowled now and, in a half angry motion, poured some Scotch into her glass and didn't bother to add soda before drinking down half of it. "Love," she said bitterly.

He looked at her, scowling himself.

"Love," she repeated. "Listen, Shell, I thought I loved both of my husbands, and it took me a long time to get over it—even after the marriages broke up."

She put down her glass abruptly, and he caught the suggestion of a choke in her voice.

"What has love got to do with it? This time there can't be any slip-ups. This time, I go into marriage with my eyes wide open. No star dust—see?" She set her mouth in determination. "This time the usually scatterbrained Sissy Patterson is being cold-blooded and sane."

"But why Mike?"

"He's in love with *me*. He represents security, Shell."

He said doggedly, "Look, this isn't any of my business, but you were telling me this morning what a rough go you had with your first two husbands. How do you know this Mike Brett-James isn't out for your money, too?"

She laughed suddenly and openly. "Shell, if I didn't know you better, didn't know how little I meant to you, I'd think you were jealous."

"What's so funny?"

She smiled at him in ridicule. "Shell, you don't know who Mike is, do you?"

"Frankly, I've never heard of him. Should I have?"

"It was a nasty thing to do, in a way," Sissy went on, "but as soon as Mike began making noises that indicated a more than passing interest, I checked back on him. This was while we were both still in Torremolinos. A cable to the London branch of my legal advisers brought a quick rundown on Michael Brett-James.

"He happens to have nearly a full page in *Burke's Peerage*, Shell. He's got so many titles he probably can't remember them all. Why, if the Plantagenets were still the ruling family of England, Mike's uncle would be king. Mike out for my money? Did you notice that ruby on his finger? It was given to a direct ancestor by the first Queen Elizabeth for gallantry against the Spanish Armada. Mike out for my money—my ridiculously small amount of money? Why Mike has a castle in Scotland that you could fit Grand Central Station into. He has a country estate in Ireland the size of a Texas cattle ranch. Mike marry me for any other reason other than that he loved me? Why, Shell, Mike's ancestors landed in England with William the Conqueror. You simply can't have a bigger name than Brett-James."

Shell Halliday had sat through all this blankly. He just didn't get it. Sissy Patterson was a superbly attractive woman, particularly sexually. He could see any *man* being strongly attracted to her.

But Mike Brett-James? The man was as queer as they came.

Shell's puzzlement must have shown in his face.

"What's the matter?" Sissy said impatiently.

He shook his head. "Nothing, I suppose. But look, you've admitted you don't really love him. What's in it for you, Sissy?"

Her voice went suddenly soft. "For me, Shell? Can't you see? The wife of Michael Brett-James. Why, when little Bunny is old enough to make her debut she'll … she'll meet the Queen, Shell. The daughter of Bootlegger Sam Patterson might not have been welcome in the better circles of Palm Beach, she might not have been eligible to attend the better finishing schools in Baltimore, but, Shell, his granddaughter will be a *lady*, in title as well as fact, after Mike legally adopts her."

Shell stared at her numbly. He shook his head again in incomprehension. He didn't have her viewpoint. Couldn't have. The things that had happened to Felicity Patterson had never, could never, have touched him. He realized that there was a bead of tear in her left eye.

Possibly he'd been wrong about Mike Brett-James. But no, that wasn't it. He'd had enough fag passes made at him to know the genuine article.

Possibly the guy was bisexual. One of these ambisexual types, whatever you called them, that liked *both* men and women. Or, for all Shell knew, possibly the guy was out for the same thing as Sissy—married respectability. And since Sissy wasn't looking for a love match, the two of them might make a go of it. She gaining her security by becoming a respected member of British society, complete with titles, he gaining his by being married and hence not suspect of his homosexual leanings.

Shell had been caught up in the conversation with the girl to the point of being unconscious of his surroundings, but now something began to intrude. A voice in the background, further down the room.

It was saying, acridly, "I have to laugh at this attitude you British have about the Anglo-American alliance. This feeling that we ought to let you have more of a say in our mutual foreign policy."

A British voice intruded then, saying something about experience and men of the caliber of Churchill.

And then the first voice bulled through again. "Churchill. He's as good an example as any. The greatest statesman of our era. Ha! Remember that speech he made once where he said belligerently that he hadn't been appointed Prime Minister to preside at the dismemberment of the British Empire? Well, that's exactly what he did. In the same half century that Churchill was a first-string leader of England, the British Empire expired. England dropped from the position of the world's first power, to being a third-rater and a stooge for Uncle Sam—a satellite. No thanks, we don't need men of Churchill's caliber."

The Englishman's voice was higher and more indignant now. "You can't say that, you bloody Yank!"

Shell Halliday was on his feet and pushing his chair back. He muttered to Sissy, who was looking at him wide-eyed, "Just a minute. Time I went into action."

He hurried to the other end of the room, his eyes seeking out and immediately locating his not inconspicuous goal.

The big cartoonist was smilingly regarding the red-faced man seated across from him. The other was wearing an RAF type mustache, arrogantly curved up on the ends, and right now he looked as though he was all set to launch into the Second Battle of Britain.

"Biggy!" Shell called. "How long have you been here?"

Bigelow Warren beamed at him drunkenly. "Shell. Where you been? I've got something for you."

Shell got him by the arm and wrestled the big man to his feet. "Pardon me," he said to the Britisher who grunted something indignantly, but who otherwise seemed to be glad to get rid of his erstwhile companion.

Shell started the cartoonist back to Sissy's table, saying, soothingly, "What've you got for me, Biggy?"

"Cashew nuts, Shell old pal. Pockets bulging with them. Very scarce in Paris."

"Great," Shell said. They'd reached Sissy. Shell said, "Biggy, here's a great admirer of yours, Miss Sissy Patterson. She's a *Bobby* fan."

"Good Heavens," Sissy said. "When Shell said he was a friend of yours, I thought he was sort of exaggerating."

Biggy leered at her and sank into a chair. "Shouldn't drink Scotch," he said. "Drink cognac."

"Why?" Sissy said.

"I forget," Bigelow told her. He fished into a pocket and brought forth a handful of cashew nuts. "Have a nut. Don't eat 'em too fast, they're hard to come by in this town." He looked at Shell accusingly. "I knew this must be Paris the minute I saw you. What day is it?"

"It's Tuesday."

Bigelow looked at him unbelievingly. "Tuesday? That's the day I arrived. It can't be Tuesday. You mean I've been here a whole week? It doesn't seem like more than two or three days."

Shell shook his head and said to Sissy, "What a guy. Some people black out when they're swacked. Some just conveniently forget anything that happens to them. But Biggy is different. He loses all sense of time."

Bigelow closed one eye and inspected Sissy with more care and with obvious approval. "You Shell's girl from Ohio?"

Sissy poured herself another drink and one for Bigelow, using Mike Brett-James' glass.

"No," she said. "I guess I'm his Florida girl."

"Boy gets around," Biggy said admiringly. "You're invited to the big party."

"What big party?" Sissy said.

"Shell and me are giving a big party for his Ohio girl when she comes. You can be a model," Bigelow leered, "gotta lotta figure."

"A lot of figure isn't exactly a flattering way of putting it," Sissy laughed. "But what's this model bit?"

"Giving old Shell a big party for this Ohio girl friend. Lots of artists. Lots of celebrities. You can be a popular model."

Her eyes went from Biggy to Shell.

"My," she said, and there was a faint hint of something beyond the mischievous in her voice. "Our laddy seems to go to considerably more trouble for his Ohio girls than for his Floridian ones."

Shell rolled his eyes upward. "Good grief," he commented.

Sissy took the hint of jealousy out of her words by laughing suddenly and saying, "Mike and I will be glad to come. He can be a titled Englishman. He can play the part fine. When is it?"

Bigelow looked at Shell accusingly. "Yeah. When is it, Shell?"

Shell said, "Don't know yet. We're not sure when she'll arrive. We'll let you know."

She looked at him obliquely and the sides of her mouth turned down. "You be sure and do that," she said. "I have an idea I'm going to like this party. It sounds interesting."

CHAPTER 5

DURING THE NEXT FEW DAYS, Shell Halliday had his work cut out for him. Cut out in such a way as for him to have suspicion at times that he was working on paper dolls. Keeping Bigelow Warren in line was strictly a job that led to the nut factory.

But it increasingly brought home to Shell just how much he loved the big, lost man.

Something, he knew, was gone out of the cartoonist's life. Something was missing. What was there that led him to compulsive drinking on a scale that sooner or later meant complete collapse? No man could stand this sort of pace. And it was accelerating. When Shell had first known Biggy, the other would throw a wingding about twice a year and it would last four or five days. But now each binge continued for as long as a month, and Bigelow was running them closer together. He'd last been in Paris less than three months ago.

He had money, Shell told himself, and he had prestige. What's more, his success was built on a stronger foundation than many these days. Bigelow Warren had a place in American satirical humor that would earn him a position ranking with such as Artemus Ward, Mark Twain and Thurber.

On top of that, everybody who met Biggy seemed to like the guy except, of course, the strangers who ran into his acid cynicism when the bear of a man was stoned. And even they, given time, would be won around by the easygoing warmth he radiated.

Shell had moved into the hotel suite as planned. The desk had been informed that the new registration was to be in the name of Shelley Halliday, and Shell's room service and other orders were to be honored as Bigelow's own. All that awaited now was the coming of Connie Lockwood. Shell figured that at soonest she'd turn up in another week or so. Meanwhile, he earned his keep as companion of Bigelow.

This evening he was having a needed but nervous holiday. Bigelow had been invited to address a banquet thrown by a club consisting of literary celebrities, members of the press corps and English-speaking diplomatic representatives. Shell knew of the Four Flushers Club, a tight-knit outfit of gourmets, wits and celebrities who met twice a month to enjoy each other's company, to eat, drink, listen to some speaker of world renown and—Shell suspected—to escape temporarily from wives and other opponents of convivial evenings.

It had taken the better part of the day to sober Biggy up to the point where he could be sent off to the banquet, in spite of the fact that the big man had a wonderful aptitude for throwing off a hangover.

But now, beyond checking his watch from time to time, Shell could relax. Earlier he had phoned the club, found that Bigelow had arrived safely, then settled back with a book and to have a few drinks on his own. He had to watch his consumption when supervising Biggy. It wouldn't do for both of them to get tight at the same time.

The bell tinkled and he yawned, put down the book and glass and made his way to the door, wondering vaguely who it could be. It was much too early for Bigelow's return.

He opened the door and frowned his lack of recognition, and then gaped. Good grief, there couldn't be this much change in just four years. No, this couldn't be Connie.

Not slightly plumpish Connie of the simple skirts and blouses, of the cotton prints, of the mere touch of lipstick in the way of make-up. Not this knockout. He had once thought her as a more rounded version of Debbie Reynolds, but this was more nearly a blond Gina Lollobrigida.

She stood for a moment, expressionless, one eyebrow raised in simulated superciliousness.

"May I come in … dahling?"

"Connie!"

"Shelley!"

They did the obviously correct thing. And even during that first, excited, hurried, inadequate kiss, Shell was conscious of the thrusting of her young breasts. Connie had evidently lost weight everywhere except there.

They found their way back into the living room and stood, staring and laughing, both talking at once, and then stood there and kissed some more.

"Wow, but you've changed. You're—" Shell stuttered.

"How in the world did you ever get this marvelous suite?"

"—for one thing, those clothes—" Shell tried to continue.

"Your mother wanted to come so badly—oh, look out, you're messing my hat—"

"I wasn't expecting you until—"

"I wanted to surprise you. Oh, Shell—"

"Hey, easy—what's the matter, Connie honey?"

"You look so different," she said. "You're messing my lipstick. You look so much older, and thinner—"

"So do you, for that matter. Wow! Little Connie has grown up."

They took time out to sit on the couch where they held hands and stared at each other, grinning inanely.

"Look," he said. "Have you got around to learning to drink?"

"Oh, I'd love one. I didn't expect you to live in Paris for years without getting beyond that occasional beer we used to have together. So, well, I took it up a little, too."

He regarded her suspiciously. "Hmmm. You sound like a fallen woman." He made his way toward Biggy's improvised bar. "What'll you have?"

"How about a rum coke?" She took her hat off and fluffed her hair. "Gosh, that Economy Class flying is a tight squeeze. I'm a rag. I suppose there's a bath with this monstrous suite."

"Two of them," Shell told her over his shoulder. He motioned with his head. "One that way, one that."

She came to her feet, her forehead worried. "Shell …?" Her voice had a new, timid quality, out of character considering her sophisticated appearance.

"I think there's Coca-Cola or Pepsi around here," he growled. "What?"

"You've got two bedrooms?"

"Yeah, that's right. Here's the coke. I'll just get some more ice out of the pantry."

"Pantry? Do you have a kitchen with this? Right in a hotel?"

"For parties and things," Shell said. She was being impressed by the layout, and Shell played it nonchalant. He had to put this over, he felt, for the sake of the people back home. He'd figure out the sequel later; there'd be someway.

Her voice was lower. "Shell. Two bedrooms. You didn't … you didn't think, just because I was coming … Shell, my parents would—"

He turned with the drink and laughed. "Don't worry, you're safe. I'll phone the desk and get you another room. Meanwhile, an old friend, Bigelow Warren, is in town and I'm putting him up. He uses the other bedroom."

"Oh." She was flustered. "Well, my bags are down in the lobby." Her neck turned pink, and she turned and went into the bedroom and beyond to the bath.

Shell put her drink down on the cocktail table near the couch and poured himself a double whiskey. He thought quickly. Connie had turned up sooner than he had figured. Was everything set for her? Bigelow, of course, was completely checked out. Shell didn't have to worry about him. It was a break that the other would be comparatively sober for his first meeting with Connie. Of course, he and Biggy hadn't got around as yet to inviting guests to the big party they'd planned for her, but that wouldn't take long. To round up a sufficient number for a party out of the crowd Shell hung around with, all you had to do was stand up at the Deux Magots or the Flore and call out, "Come on, everybody, a party at my place." Of course, for this one they'd have to be more discriminating.

Shell checked his wallet quickly. He was in abnormally good financial shape. Bigelow made a point each evening, before they started out, of handing Shell a couple of hundred francs for reserve money so that his companion could pay part of the bills and avoid appearing to be a free-loader. Biggy was thoughtful about such things. Besides that, Shell had few expenses living here at the George Fifth and taking his meals with the cartoonist or merely putting them on the hotel's tab. He even still had some of the money that he'd got that evening he took Sissy on her pub crawl.

His mind raced. This wasn't going to be as simple as Bigelow had contended. Shell had a double problem. He'd have to keep watch on the cartoonist and at the same time he'd have to spend time with Connie. He was going to be hard put to keep the girl from wondering why he didn't spend all his hours with her, instead of pub-crawling with Bigelow.

He snapped his fingers. With Bigelow accounted for at the Four Flushers Club, he could safely take the time to escort her out for dinner. Bigelow would be out until late and Shell would even have time for a few night spots. He'd better do it tonight, while he had the chance.

Connie returned, her face fresher, her make-up new. She said, "Did you say Bigelow Warren?"

"That's right," Shell said.

"You mean the man who does *Bobby*?"

Shell poured himself another drink, handed her hers. "Yeah, that's Biggy," he said casually.

Connie was impressed. "And he's staying here with you?"

"That's right. Look, Connie, have you eaten?"

"On the plane."

"Economy class? Terrible. Let's go out and have a bite. You're not too tired, are you? We could have the hotel send up something."

"Oh, Shell, let's go to one of those bistros you're always writing about." All of a sudden it all seemed to come home to her. She was with Shell again. She was in Paris. Paris!—where everything was allegedly beautiful, sparkling and young. Where there were no troubles and humanity's grossness sloughed away, snake-skin-like.

He struck a pose. "A bistro it is. We'll find the most wonderful bistro in Paris! For Connie Lockwood's first meal in the city of gourmets!"

She took up his spirit. Arm in arm they marched from the suite and, ignoring the elevators, down the curved stairway, through the ornate lobby—to a salute of grins from both hotel employees and guests at their obvious joy in life—and to the street.

"A cab, Monsieur Halliday?" Nicolas said, dead pan. The former Cossack had seen *joie de vivre* sail forth into the sea of Paris before, usually returning in the wee hours in the form of a hangover.

"A cab, Nicolas? Fie on you. On such a glorious night?" Shell demanded loftily.

Connie giggled. Oh, this was Paris, all right.

They swept on.

* * * *

In a fashion, it was a duplication of the evening he'd spent not too long ago with Sissy Patterson and Mike Brett-James. It hadn't started off that way. He'd had in mind an excellent but unostentatious meal in one of the spots he truly appreciated, one of the minor restaurants untouched by the expensive tourist finger, possibly in the Halles district, or the Sorbonne section where the food and wine would be good and the atmosphere conducive to murmured conversation.

It hadn't started that way, but Shell got caught up in the driving need to prove himself. To prove himself in the eyes of a girl who needed no proof? No. Face it. His need was to prove himself to Shell Halliday. Somehow to make him feel that he was important, that he deserved the shine in Connie Lockwood's eyes.

Possibly Nicolas the doorman had started it with his courtly bow and his air of deference to Monsieur Halliday. Nicolas, who greeted kings and presidents, oil millionaires and movie stars, sultans from Arabia and industrial tycoons from West Germany, and headline politicians from the world over. Yes, possibly Nicolas had started it all.

Hardly had they got out of earshot of that weary doorman, who couldn't have cared less, than Connie looked up at her escort. "How in the world can he possibly remember the names of the guests at such a big hotel?"

Shell laughed at her and squeezed her arm. "Darling, you're an innocent. He couldn't begin to. Only ... only the names of us old-timers. I've been coming to the George Fifth, off and on, for years now." Which was true enough. Bigelow Warren invariably stayed at the ultra-swank hotel and many a time had Shell brought him home in the early hours, to be helped by Nicolas in the final stages of getting Biggy safely to the elevator and to his suite.

So instead of the little bistro in the Halles district, they wound up in one of the currently popular tourist traps and, as always where Shell had his contacts, he was given the red carpet treatment. The doorman bowed, the headwaiter simpered, a captain came arunning. Pavillon Paris might not boast the food quality of some, but the Pavillon did have *service*.

Connie was properly impressed. She was impressed by Shell's royal greeting, by his conference with Marcel pertaining to the evening's repast and the gobbledygook palaver with the wine steward. Nor did she notice when the bill came that the headwaiter raised his eyebrows to Shell in question before handing the check to him rather than to her.

She was doubly impressed in a Montparnasse club afterwards when the entertainers spoke to Shell and the chanteuse stopped long enough for a drink at their table.

The town knew Shell, all right, and the fact that most of them snickered behind the scenes could hardly be known to Connie. Shell had another sucker on the string. Build him up, play the game. When Shell found a live one, you could depend on getting away with padding the bill, on high tips, and on the good chance that the tourist would return again, often with friends.

It was a hilarious time. With his pencil, on the tablecloth, Shell did snide, cruel, hilariously funny caricatures of the entertainers, the waiters, and the other habitués of the club. Connie could hardly refrain from screaming laughter. Ah, but this was Paris!

It was in the intimacy of the tiny Vieux Caveau, over early-morning champagne, and to the strains of Vietnamese music accompanying the tiny Indo-Chinese stripper that Connie decided what she must do.

She looked at Shell pensively. He was watching the tiny, delicate Oriental dancer with obvious lack of interest. The art of disrobing, which originated so long ago in the bump-and-grind school of American burlesque, had been raised to pinnacles in the work of such competent performers as this. But it was obviously old hat to Shell.

Connie, who had seen one or two of the more discreet strippers in the Cincinnati night spots and those across the river in Newport, Kentucky, was surprised at his obvious disinterest. The girl was surpassingly exotic, her curves so dainty as to be doll-like. Connie couldn't conceive of any man not being aroused by the provocative sweetness of the dancer's display. The tiny, coral-tipped breasts, so small but so perfect; the gentle swell of hips, the tiny, tiny waist.

Connie gasped suddenly. "Why—why, is she going to take *everything* off?"

Shell stifled a yawn and grinned at her. "Probably," he said. "About once a week, if there are no police around, Pierre allows Li to shoot the works. Keeps the customers coming back. Cute little trick, isn't she?"

Just at that moment, the cute little trick paraded arrogantly past their table. She winked an Oriental eye at them and said, low in her throat, "'Allo, Shell," and passed on. The last time Shell had been in the Vieux Caveau he'd brought three heavy-spending, expense-account executives and one of them had stuffed a hundred-dollar bill in the rear elastic of her ultra-abbreviated

G-string. It hadn't felt particularly comfortable there but Li was willing to put up with a degree of discomfort for the sake of that much money.

Had Shell known it, Li's greeting sent his prestige to its zenith for that evening.

Connie reached her moment of truth.

She had wondered these past years why Shell hadn't returned for her. Or, at least, why he hadn't sent for her. As his success, as reported in his letters, had grown and grown again, as he began to move in the circles of the great, his letters had fallen off and something, well, *intimate* had gone out of them.

Frankly, Connie had regretted that she hadn't yielded that last night in the car when Shell had pressed her so hard. That night when she had almost—but not quite. Had she permitted him the ultimate favor, surely he would have been bound to her.

Yes, this was her moment of truth.

Of course, the drinks helped. The two Cuba Libras she'd had at the suite before they started out, the several types of wine at the restaurant and the after-dinner liqueur. Then the champagne they'd had in one nightery after the other. Connie was no prude and no teetotaler, but she'd never been more than moderately tipsy in her life. Yes, the alcohol helped.

Reality flooded her. Why, her Shell could have any woman in the place, including that slinky little Chinese—or whatever she was—strip-teaser.

Shell, who had once been pleased with the bounty of Connie's kisses, an occasionally fondled breast, a moist nervous palm pressed mometarily over her knee, had probably known a dozen women since then. Possibly even more, many more, in these past four years.

And Connie? What was the word? *Square?* No, that was passé now. *Corny*, they used to say when she was a little girl, and then *square*, and now they had one of these new beatnik words, but she was too fuzzy to remember. She took another defiant gulp of her bubbling wine.

In a way it was Shell's fault. She'd kept herself for him. Not just her body, but her *self*. Possibly she'd overdone it. Possibly it would have been better had she seen a little more of life, got to know other men. She felt almost ridiculous. She had prided herself on maintaining her virginity, saving her body for Shell. But now the question arose—did he want it? Had she been a fool to preserve something undesired? Perhaps, in his new sophistication, Shell was contemptuous of the old values, such as a woman's virginity at marriage. Just what purpose *did* it serve?

Connie took another long pull at her champagne.

Oh, she'd been out a few times, not only with the gang and on double dates, but alone with men. She'd even done a certain amount of necking, but everybody in her circle knew she was Shell's and saving herself for Shell.

And after a time, most of her male acquaintances had given her up as a lost cause. It hadn't helped her popularity.

She looked at him from the side of her eyes. And now he seemed a stranger, she thought. Had the waiting been worth it? She forced down her momentary feeling of doubt. Don't be a fool, Constance Lockwood, this is the man you've wanted since you were a teen-ager. Of course, there were some changes in him. *The trouble is, there aren't enough changes in you,* she told herself. *Here, while he was accumulating experiences, growing in sophistication, you were becoming an old maid in New Elba. Face it, Constance Lockwood. You're downright old-fashioned.*

Unconsciously, Connie ran a hand down over her right breast and as far as the hip and thigh, as though checking her natural attributes. She wasn't dismayed. Connie was normally vain, normally curious and normally conscious of her sex values. The full-length mirror in her room at home had told her that she had little to fear in the competition between womankind for the tribute of the male.

She took another gulp of the wine and let Shell fill her glass again.

He looked at her narrowly. Actually, Shell himself, relieved of the tension of riding herd on Bigelow Warren, and building himself up in the eyes of Connie, had been hitting the bottle considerably more than was his wont. In fact, he hadn't let himself go this far for a long time, he realized. It was time he got them both back to the hotel.

Connie wet her lips and eyed him strangely.

"What's the matter, Connie?" he asked.

Connie Lockwood cleared her throat. She said abruptly, "Let's go back to the hotel, Shelley."

There was something in her voice that Shell couldn't quite put his finger on, but he shrugged inwardly. He'd been thinking the same thing himself, that it was time to go. Among other things, he was just about flat broke. He poured the balance of the champagne into their glasses.

"To us!" he toasted.

She held up her glass in silent repetition of the toast, and there was grim determination in her eyes as they looked into his.

Connie had decided to give her all.

* * * *

It isn't that easy for a girl to yield herself to a man who for long years has thought of her as untouchable, who respects her and expects to make her his wife.

In a way, Connie had a problem on her hands. One doesn't just come out and say, "Dear, we've been going together since high school and now we're in our late twenties. I've decided to give you what you've wanted all these years."

No, you couldn't exactly put it that way.

What you could do is accept the nightcap he gave you and lean back on the couch while he phoned the desk for a room which you were supposedly going to occupy. You could work yourself into as advantageous a position as occurred to you—advantageous, that is, so far as exploiting your more desirable attributes. You could lower your lashes in a manner most successfully exploited on the screen by Miss Sophia Loren and wait.

She realized that she should put the drink aside, that she'd had plenty, but she needed the excuse not to go to her own room. And she needed the courage it gave her.

The room secured, Shell rejoined her, his own nightcap in hand.

He grinned at Connie. "Have a good time?"

"Oh, wonderful. I was just sitting here laughing at those silly drawings of yours. That one you did of the fat master of ceremonies."

Her mouth was comfortably available for kissing. He kissed her. At this stage, Shell Halliday could never have admitted it, not even to himself, but something had gone out of kissing Connie. It wasn't what it had once been in New Elba. Why, he didn't even think to analyze, but actually Connie's fears were justified. Shell had developed a taste for sophistication in his love-making.

But they kissed, and kissed again, and no man is as strong as all that. Somehow her skirt was above her knees by the time he got up to refreshen their glasses. He turned the light low before returning. They each half emptied their drinks before going back to where they'd left off. The skirt had not been readjusted.

About this time, in his liquor-loosened mind, Shell realized that tonight Connie would be his. In spite of her earlier protests when she'd thought he expected her to share this suite with him, Connie was his for the taking. Had he been more sober, he would have been more surprised. As it was, he accepted the new state of affairs without too much examination. He was too far gone in liquor to appraise anything too clearly.

Her jacket was off now, and her blouse unbuttoned. He gently tugged away the garment beneath and Connie's breasts, almost forgotten in the years between, were his to appreciate, with his eyes and his hands. Her head was back, her face pale, her eyes closed, as he toyed with her—expertly.

His experience took control, over the alcohol-bewildered self-censor. Shell bent his head and placed his mouth to a nipple. She drew her breath in sharply and muttered a meaningless negation.

She was beyond control now. Connie, for a decade and more, had been capable of the act of love and desirous of it. And Connie was that now rarely met item, a beautiful woman who has passed her mid-twenties, a virgin. Nature boiled uncontrollably within her.

She sat suddenly erect, taking his head in her hands. She was trembling. "Oh no, don't do that. Don't do that any more."

He looked up at her, his eyes dreamily sloe.

She said, "Wait. Wait just a moment. I … I'll call you, darling."

Somewhere she'd read that, the way to do it on the first night—on the wedding night, the honeymoon. The bride went into the bedroom and promised to call when she was ready.

Connie came to her feet and made her way to the nearest of the two bedrooms. She stopped at the door and looked back, her face flaming in embarrassment. "I'll call you when I'm ready," she promised again.

He stared after her, then shook his head to achieve clarity. He'd drunk *considerably* more than he'd thought.

But what he needed now, desperately, was another drink. The stuff was dying in him. He needed another good stiff one to bring him around. There definitely was something missing in the situation and he hoped to find out what after one more drink.

He wavered his way to the sideboard, took up the bottle of Metaxa, the Greek brandy, and poured himself a stiff one. It would have been jolt enough had it been the comparatively low proof French cognac, but Metaxa is distilled with heroes in mind. He tossed it back, stared down into the glass in approval, and poured another double shot to carry back to the couch with him.

Heavens to Betsy, after all these years it was going to be Connie. He and Connie, the first girl who'd really made him conscious of the world of relationship between men and women. Connie, who even at the age of fifteen had been capable of stirring him to the point where he'd lay in bed at night, staring at the ceiling, with beads of sweat on his face as his body demanded hers.

Well, tonight Connie, at long last, was to be his.

He could hear her stirring in the next room. He tossed back the Metaxa. That was Connie in there, his Connie, at long last.

He wished he wasn't so tired. If he'd known this was coming up, he wouldn't have hit the bottle so hard.

He let his head fall to the soft back of the couch and closed his eyes— for a moment. So at last it was going to be Connie.

* * * *

Bigelow Warren shut one eye and zeroed in on the keyhole of the door. The elevator boy had offered to see him to his suite but Biggy had denied his assistance with considerable dignity. He didn't consider himself drunk—not by Bigelow Warren's standards. He was just, say, pleasantly fuzzy. Yep, that was the word. Pleasantly fuzzy.

What was it the newspaperman had said tonight at the Four Flushers? Oh, yeah. "Hell, he's not drunk, I just saw him move."

What he meant was, the proof was right before his eyes—he couldn't be drunk, otherwise he couldn't have got this here key in the lock. *There. That's proof, isn't it? There's proof for you.*

Brother, did those characters at the Four Flushers pour it down. Newspapermen. And those diplomats. Ha, diplomats. He'd have to work something into *Bobby* about diplomats. No wonder they fouled up the world the way they did. Who wouldn't with the kinda hangovers those boozers must have?

The door swung open.

The apartment was but dimly lit. Old Shell, good old Shell, must have gone to bed. Well, this was one night he'd got along without his good old seeing-eye dog, Shell. Got back to the hotel all by hisself, didn't he?

He wove into the living room. He deserved a drink. Gave a brilliant talk to the boys tonight. Had them all sick to the stomach laffing so hard. Glad he stuck to cognac. Now, no hangover in the morning. Good old Jerry Whatever-his-name-was, in Philly, had told him about cognac. No hangover. Trouble was, he usually forgot to stick to it after he'd had a few. But tonight he had. He'd told the bartender at the Four Flushers not to give him anything but cognac, no matter what he ordered.

He stared at the couch.

"Be damned," Biggy muttered. He nudged the other. Shell snored on, his mouth slack. "Out like a light," Bigelow muttered. "Don't believe I ever saw old Shell really stoned before."

He shrugged and headed for the sideboard, feeling strangely lifted that he was still on his feet while Shell was out.

A voice from the bedroom pulled him up sharp.

"I'm ready, darling."

Bigelow blinked.

He looked back at the collapsed figure of his friend on the couch, then at the bedroom door.

Then he grumbled inner laughter. Old Shell had picked himself up one of those Left Bank semipros, most likely, and brought her back to the suite. Bigelow wondered how he'd ever managed to smuggle her past the desk. The George Fifth was touchy about such.

"Darling," the voice slurred from the inner room. "I'm ready."

Lord, she *sounded* ready. She sounded as though she'd put away a few herself. Probably not an out-and-out professional, just one of those ultra-loose-living friends of Shell's.

Bigelow came to a sudden decision, chuckling. He slipped out of his coat and tossed it aside. He noted Shell had already discarded his tie and that his shirt was unbuttoned halfway down. Biggy did the same.

Then he went toward the bedroom door. He hoped the light had been turned off inside, otherwise it would never work.

It was off, all right, and Connie, without even a nightgown in the way of protection, had regained a portion of her fears.

As she felt his weight settle to the side of the bed, she murmured, "Oh, darling, be … be gentle."

"Ummm," he said, reaching for her."

She realized briefly, faintly, that it shouldn't have been this way, that they should never have decided upon this while they had been drinking. It was such a shame—the first time—to have been drinking.

But she was ready for him. She needed him so badly. So many years to wait for what your body wanted, demanded for its fulfillment.

He buried his face in her neck, and she could feel him nibble gently. She could feel his hands going everywhere, everywhere over her body. She wondered now if she shouldn't have left some faint light on. But no, it would have been too embarrassing.

In the back of her mind was a faint, faint disturbing thought. Shell seemed so large. She must really be drunk because she had thought earlier that he'd lost weight. But he seemed so big, so masculine. She smiled faintly to herself. She had nothing to compare this experience to—it was the first time she'd ever been in bed with a man.

And she was enjoying it—no, that was too mild a word—she was loving it, loving it, loving it …

She felt the strong hands taking up the manipulation of her breasts, she felt the mouth encircling a nipple and she sighed deeply, remembering that that's where they had left off before—before she had broken away to prepare herself for this first time, this wedding night … the honeymoon.

Now she knew that she had missed a great deal.

A hand moved to her thigh, kneading, building a fire within her.

"Oh, yes … yes …" she murmured and, involuntarily, her hand moved to encourage further and bolder intrusion. Her other hand sought her lover—oh, Shell, Shell—and she thrilled with her inordinate boldness.

There was a sudden shifting of bodies, a protest from the bedsprings and she had a moment of returning panic.

And then the sharp pain came, and she forgot about everything, particularly when the pain fell away in such a brief moment and she arched her hips up, receiving, and all was movement and straining.

Vaguely, at the last moment, she thought, *Shell should really take off some weight. Appearances are certainly deceiving.*

Bigelow Warren awoke first in the morning. In fact, he had slept no more than two or three hours. When Bigelow was on the sauce he took his sleep, as he did his eating, philosophically. One time he'd sleep twenty hours through, again he'd go for forty-eight without touching a bed.

He lay for a moment, staring up at the ceiling, not fully tight but still with alcohol's grasp upon him. He tried to orient himself in time and location. He was drunk, so he must be in Paris. Yeah, but what was the time?— or the date, for that matter?

He was conscious of a girl beside him, and part of the evening before came back to him. He was in his George Fifth suite and he'd pulled a joke on old Shell, laying the tart Shell had brought up to the suite.

The room, its shades pulled, was still murkily dark. Moving as carefully as possible, he rolled from the bed. Behind him, the girl stirred in her sleep. The big cartoonist grinned and, taking up his clothes, tiptoed to the door and into the living room.

Shell was still out like a light.

Bigelow, highly amused by the situation, dressed silently and, still tiptoeing, went to the door and let himself out. He had a picture in his mind of Shell and the girl awakening later, and the girl demanding her pay while Shell denied he'd run up a bill.

* * * *

Connie shook him.

"Shell. Shell darling, what are you doing out here?"

He came awake blearily and squinted up at her. She was completely dressed in her clothes of the day before.

He shook his head for clarity, swung his feet around and to the floor. His head was pounding.

He looked up at her again, pursing his lips. "Wow, I feel awful."

She seemed embarrassed for some reason or another. As though to cover up, she put a hand to her forehead and said, "And *me!* I've never, *never* drunk so much in all my life."

"I'll have them send up some coffee and tomato juice," Shell offered. He stood and walked over to the phone, moaning complaints.

Connie said, hurriedly, "But … but what will they think? I mean, my spending the night here?"

He picked up the phone. "Oh, did you? Didn't you get to your room at all? Wow. I've done some drinking in my time, but I don't ever remember going this far. I spent the whole night there on the couch."

She stared at him. "But, darling—"

"Oh, don't worry about the service," he continued, unaware of her reaction to his truthful statement. "For one thing, this is Paris, and they couldn't care less. For another, you're completely dressed—they have no way of knowing."

Into the phone he said, "Breakfast for two, please. Lots of tomato juice."

Her eyes were wide. "But darling …"

He frowned at her. "What's the matter, Connie?"

"But … well, last night."

"What about last night? Admittedly we overdid, but—"

"But, *darling* … you and me."

Now he was staring. Frankly, he couldn't remember going to sleep, nor the details of their last moments together. "What's the matter, Connie?"

She was aghast. "But darling, we—" Suddenly she had slumped to the couch he had occupied a moment before and her head was in her hands. "Now you don't want me," she said. "I … I shouldn't have let you. Now you don't want me. Now you'll never marry me."

He didn't get it. He didn't begin to get it. He shook his head and said, "Wait a minute, honey. Let me throw some cold water on my face."

He went into the bedroom she'd occupied the night before and headed for the bath. But he got no further than halfway through the room before his eyes hit the rumpled condition of the bed. He stopped abruptly, did a double-take and understanding flooded over him. The meaning of Connie's confusion hit him.

There was no question about Connie Lockwood having been a virgin.

He stumbled on into the bath, turned on the cold water and splashed his face repeatedly, his mind churning. He couldn't remember it at all. Not at all. He couldn't remember anything about it.

Shell looked at himself in the mirror. His face was whiter than the after-effects of the night before warranted. This really tore it.

When he got back to the living room, Connie was sitting in one of the great chairs, her hands in her lap and her expression drawn. Her eyes were blinking, as though she were keeping tears back at considerable effort.

"I'm sorry, honey," Shell told her.

"Sorry," she said blankly.

"I mean. Well, when I first awoke, I had forgotten. I guess I was pretty tight."

"But Shelley," she said in a rush. "I … I don't know much about such things … but, aren't you supposed to do something … or me? I mean—" Her face was flaming now and she put both hands to it. "A *baby* …" she wailed.

Oh, good grief. He sat on the arm of her chair and put an arm around her. "Now honey …"

"Shelley, Shelley, we can't put it off any longer now. We ... we will be *married*, won't we?"

She wasn't able to see his face, so he allowed himself to cast his eyes upward in defeat.

Married! He, Shell Halliday, married? Why, he was in no more position to be married than—than what? He couldn't think of a comparison. It was just out, out of the question. Damn it, he needed time to think. What had got into him last night? Was he so stupid as not to realize that with girls like Connie these things were dead serious and for keeps? Not just a roll in the hay to be forgotten the day after.

Married? Why, even given everything else, given a job, given a life worth the sharing, given everything that *Connie* needed to be happy in a marriage—how about him? Sure, as a high school kid, even during his college years, it was all Connie. But he wasn't a student any more, he wasn't a New Elba pseudo-artist any longer. He was the product of almost five years of hard living in the most cynically sophisticated city in the world. Was he interested in marriage to anyone at all? And, if so, was Connie the one?

He didn't know. He simply didn't know.

Meanwhile, her overly obvious distress, her real grief and fear was tearing him down. He wasn't a heel, he told himself; he'd never been a heel.

He got only part of what she was saying between sobs. If she'd only stop for a moment and let him get his bearings.

He patted her shoulder uncomfortably, "Sure, Connie, of course. Don't cry."

"You mean ... you mean you *did* plan to marry me?"

Oh Lord, what had he said?

Well, was he a heel, or wasn't he? The chips were down.

He patted her shoulder. "Sure, honey, of course."

The emotional storm passed away magically. She was suddenly radiant and enthusiastic. "Oh, darling, how in the world can we announce our engagement over here? I don't know anybody."

He licked dry lips. He wished Bigelow was around to advise him again. What had he gotten into? It was far, far too late now. He had to have time to think. To make some sort of *plan*. He had to get out of this situation.

While his mind raced, seeking an avenue of escape that didn't present itself, he was saying soothingly, "Bigelow Warren and I have been planning a special party for you, honey. Lots of my friends."

She was as pleased as a child, he thought glumly. If she'd suddenly begun clapping her hands and jumping up and down, he wouldn't have been too surprised. That patina of sophistication she'd worn yesterday hadn't proved to go very deep.

"When? Oh, Shelley, I'll have to buy a special dress."

"They have a few here in Paris," he said wryly.

She was on her feet now, radiant. The fears and tears of a moment before were gone as the snows of yesteryear. "When is it to be?"

"Oh, we were waiting for you to show up. Tomorrow night, I suppose. We can arrange it for tomorrow."

CHAPTER 6

HE HAD TO FIND BIGELOW. First of all, he had to talk to *somebody* and Bigelow Warren was the only friend he could think of. Besides wanting advice on his present situation with Connie, Shell was worried about the burly cartoonist. The idea had been that the other was to return immediately to the George Fifth after the Four Flushers Club banquet.

He'd expected Bigelow to do some drinking at the affair, but the other had assured him that he'd return to the suite before taking off for any further rounds of the town. And you could usually trust Bigelow, even when drinking, to abide by a promise.

The trouble probably was that the big man had gotten mixed up again in time and location. He probably figured it was a week earlier than reality—or even a week later. After a certain point, Biggy could manage to lose track of what year it was.

Connie was gone. Off to the Champs Elysées shops to find a party dress, one suitable for announcing their engagement in. There was a double element in the distress he felt about her. He could hardly admit it to himself, but somehow the feeling for Connie wasn't the same. The years had done something to the relationship. Attractive she was, more than ever, but … well, something seemed gone.

It was pushing toward noon. He and Connie had slept late after the heavy drinking and late hours of the night before.

He racked his brains. Where would Bigelow be this time of day? He had no idea if the cartoonist had been drinking steadily since the night before, or if he'd holed up somewhere, either with a friend, one of the new contacts he'd made at the Four Flushers Club last evening, or with some streetwalker. Shell well knew that after a few days of drinking, Bigelow Warren would often develop a taste for a woman—and by Shell's standards, his taste wasn't very good.

That was one of the things Shell had often wondered about in his cartoonist friend. Bigelow seemed to have little, if any, interest in the charms of the women he came in contact with in either his business or his social life. Oh, he was courteous enough, charming enough—everybody liked Biggy— but even those women who made the most obvious plays for the big man, never seemed to get anywhere.

Not that there seemed to be anything wrong in that department. He operated lustily enough with the professionals you could pick up around Pigalle at night or in the vicinity of the Madeleine in the afternoon.

But the question now was, where in the devil was the man?

It was a question which had presented itself before, all too often, and Shell went into his routine. He phoned those bars where he knew the help was acquainted with Warren—and drew a blank. That was bad. He was hoping the other was at Harry's New York Bar, Fred Payne's in Montmartre, or possibly the Flore or the Deux Magots in the St. Germain des Prés section.

He snapped his fingers. That's where Bigelow might be. At the Lipp, right across the street from the Deux Magots. It was an Alsatian bar-restaurant with some of the best brew in town. The idea was to order a *sérieux*, a gigantic glass of beer, and to sit at a table on the sidewalk and watch the world go by. By nursing, you could drag out a *sérieux* for the whole afternoon. Not that Bigelow was ever the nursing type drinker, but it was a hot afternoon and this was the one time of day Biggy drank beer.

No use phoning the Lipp, it wasn't the kind of place where the manager was apt to know a customer by name. The American celebrity would be just one more tourist.

Shell went up to the Franklin D. Roosevelt station on the Pont Neuilly-Vincennes metro line and took the subway to the Chatelet station, where he transferred to the Porte d'Orléans line, finally getting off at St. Germain des Prés in front of the Abbey.

He crossed the street, nodded at a couple of acquaintances sunning themselves before the Deux Magots, and then crossed St. Germain to the Lipp.

Shell had hit it on the button. There was Bigelow, weaving slightly in his chair, an amiable grin on his face, a half empty glass of dark Alsatian beer before him. He was seated at a table nearest to the passers-by and one of the waiters was eying him sadly. Biggy was obviously completely soused and no advertisement for the Lipp.

Shell slipped into a chair across from him. "Hi, Biggy," he said.

"Shell, old boy," Bigelow Warren said. "Where you been? I knew I was in Paris, all right, all right, because I'm drunk and I haven't got drunk anywhere but in Paris in the past five years. This *is* Paris, isn't it? They got sidewalk cafés in Rome, too, you know. Yep, it must be Paris because you live in Paris. What's the date, Shell?"

Shell told him. It didn't seem to make much of an impression on the big cartoonist.

"Look, Bigelow, remember I told you about my girl coming?" Shell asked.

"Yep. We sure fixed that, didn't we?"

"Not yet, Biggy. We're *going* to fix it," Shell said patiently.

The other looked at him apologetically. "I guess I'm mixed up, Shell. I thought we handled that a month or so ago."

"Come on, Biggy, we're going to the *sauna*," Shell told him.

The other was hurt. "You mean that overgrown steam bath where the female wrestler comes in while you're stark naked and beats the bejazus out of you with a bundle of thorns?"

"Twigs," Shell said, standing up. "Come on, Biggy, there's an emergency and I have to talk to you. Fact is, I can use some sobering up myself."

The cartoonist wavered to his feet. "If it's an emergency, old pal of mine, old faithful watchdog, I'm game for anything—even a Finnish bath."

* * * *

Finland's contribution to the bath gives indication why the Finns, back in the late Thirties, were able to hold off the military might of the Soviet Union for long months. This Finn institution, indulged in at least once each day in the year, is only for the strong. None other could survive its rigors. It makes all other national baths, from the Roman and the Turkish to the Japanese, take a back seat. These were child's play. And it is absolutely guaranteed to soak as much as a couple of weeks of accumulated alcohol from the body of the lushest lush who ever bent an elbow.

Shell and Bigelow sat on wooden benches in the *sauna* steam room in the Hôtel Helsinki, off the Boulevard des Capucines. The management had gone to some effort to create the Finnish atmosphere and it took little imagination to believe that outside would be a bleak Northern vista, complete with pines and an ice-cold lake in which to dip after the bath.

Bigelow, sweat running in rivulets from every pore in his heavy body, growled unhappily, "I can't imagine anybody paying to have this done to them. Somehow, I always have the idea in my head that the owners of this hell-hole are sadists and ought to pony up for the pleasure of committing this assault on our persons."

Shell grinned at him. "The only reason I come here, Biggy, is to watch the horrified look spread over your face when that muscular buffalo of a woman comes in with the birch branch and begins to whale away at you."

Biggy glowered at him in indignation. "I suspect it's a put-up job. They don't really do this to themselves in Finland."

"No," Shell said. "It's the real thing. Supposed to speed up the circulation and the cleansing effect of the *sauna*. Of course, this place is comparatively on the mild side. All they've got is a cold swimming pool when we're finished in here. Up in Finland they run outside and roll in the snow, or chop a hole in the ice and dive into the lake."

Bigelow shuddered.

Later, the steam bath over, the two relaxed in easy chairs in the Helsinki lounge. Although they'd put away approximately half a gallon each of ice water, to counter the dehydrating effect of the ultra-hot steam bath, they both felt the need of a long cold beer and were feeling a self-satisfied martyrdom over refraining.

The cartoonist growled, "I think that big wench has it in for me. She gave me twice the beating she did you. I think she left marks on my bottom."

Shell observed him critically. "I don't know. It's just that you *look* like you need a beating. Any normal woman, with a normal mother's instinct, would probably like to take a switch to you."

"Very funny," Biggy grumbled. "Okay, so you've got me sobered up, a fate worse than debt. Now what? What's the big crisis?"

Shell went serious. It suddenly occurred to him that he couldn't tell his friend the whole story. Bigelow, when drinking, could get himself too confused to be trustworthy. However, the whole truth wasn't necessary.

He said, "Look, Biggy, Connie has arrived and … well, we're engaged. She wants to announce it at the party."

"Great," Biggy said. "That'll be the climax of the evening. Yep, we'll announce the engagement."

Shell glared at him. "A lot of help you are."

"What's the matter? What's the big crisis? Nothing has happened. You were sort of semi-engaged to her anyway, weren't you?"

"Well, yes. But, look, this is serious. More definite."

The big cartoonist shrugged his shoulders. "I don't see why. The same situation applies. We'll make arrangements for a telegram to come the day after the party. Big job painting a mural in Senegal. Connie has to go back to the States. Everything is solved. She'll go on back to Ohio and tell everybody you're on top of the world in Paris. Engagements can be broken. Later on you'll break this one by mail."

Shell slumped deeper into his chair. He wondered what the other would say if he revealed that Shell had bedded the girl the night before. It some ways, Bigelow was all but puritanical in his outlook. But no, he couldn't tell even this friend of his. It would accomplish nothing.

And Bigelow Warren was right. Nothing basic had changed. Connie's fear of having a baby was probably nonsense. He couldn't remember if he had taken any precautions or not, but pregnancy usually isn't as easy as all that. Comparatively few brides conceive on their wedding nights.

If she was pregnant, then he could start plans from there—maybe go back to New Elba and take his medicine. Certainly he wasn't heel enough to desert the girl.

Biggy was saying, "When should we hold the party, Shell?"

"I told her tomorrow." He looked at the cartoonist. "If that's okay with you, Biggy. I still think you're going far, far beyond the call of duty on this."

"Nonsense. I think it's great. A lot of fun. But we'd better start getting organized. I'll go on back to the hotel and make arrangements for catering the party. Liquor and everything. You'd better start drumming up some impressive guests. Don't forget Manfred." Bigelow came to his feet, preparatory to going.

"Manfred who?"

"The waiter at the Flore."

Shell stood, too. "Oh, old Manfred. Why shouldn't I forget that fallen-arched old—"

"His full name is Manfred von Nauheim und zur Lüneburg and he's a grand duke," Biggy said with dignity. "Used to have his own duchy in the old days. When he's done up for the occasional party he gets invited to, usuually by somebody he knew in the past, he looks like a Bulgarian rear admiral—very impressive."

"Live and learn," Shell said. "I've known Manfred for years. Always complaining about his feet. Okay, he's in. Has he got a duchess?"

"He was telling me the last time I was in town. She left him to marry a prince."

"A prince, yet!"

"Well, a Hungarian prince. Has a job as a taxi driver these days."

Shell laughed spontaneously. "It just occurs to me that this is going to be some party. I'll have to invite Jan Luchtvaart. He's the artiest-looking artist who ever lived. And he can make with more art gobbledygook talk than any other man on earth."

"Yep," Biggy said. "Only shortcoming is that Jan shouldn't be allowed to paint barns. Well, let's get going. I'll head back for the hotel. Oh yeah, don't forget Dave Shepherd. I saw him around last night, or last week, or whenever it was."

"Ummm," Shell said. "Dave is the most Bohemian-looking—whatever that is—queer in Paris. He *looks* authentic. If he's not a real, honest-to-goodness Bohemian, nobody is."

Bigelow laughed. His hangover was forgotten and he was beginning to enjoy this. But he had a serious moment before taking leave of Shell.

"Listen, Shell," he said. "Don't let this get you down. It can't be as important, really, as all that."

Shell frowned at him. "Why not? It's pretty damned important."

Biggy shook his head and grinned slyly. "This Connie can't mean as much as all that to you. If she did you wouldn't have had that tart up in the room last week, or whenever it was."

Tart? Shell was about to ask the big man what he was talking about but gave up the idea. Biggy undoubtedly had his time twisted again and was possibly referring to something that had happened during the last binge he'd been on here in Paris. Shell was beginning to worry seriously about the other's mental health. At this rate, he'd be taking the cure in some sanitarium before the year was out.

He said simply, "Okay, Biggy, see you later."

* * * *

Back at the George Fifth, Bigelow Warren sternly avoided even looking at his imposing array of bottles on the sideboard and took up the phone. Even while he was still making arrangements for a lavish supply of food and drink for the following night, a bartender, waiter, and the other needs of the party, there was a tinkling of the bell.

He said into the phone. "That'll be it for the time being, Walter. If there's anything else I think of, I'll call again."

He put the phone down and went to the suite's entry. There was a girl there and Biggy, his mind on the catering, was blank for a moment.

He had the damnedest feeling that he'd met her somewhere before, although that seemed unlikely. He couldn't have forgotten a girl this distinctive. And for a moment she cocked her head to one side, frowning slightly, as though she, too, were trying to establish some connection between them. It was as if something psychic had passed between them—and then was gone.

She was, he would estimate, somewhere in her mid-twenties. Blond, but not too blond, her crowning glory a gift of nature rather than something bought at the beauty parlor. She was moderately tall and immoderately well endowed with curves, dips and contours. Her face was excellent, open, clean, direct of eye. By all the criteria that counted in Bigelow Warren's book, she was a beauty. Nor did she have to open her mouth for him to know she was an American. Only the States turned out that healthy feminine type known unkindly as corn-fed Midwestern.

It came to him suddenly who she was. "You're Connie," he exclaimed and smiled broadly.

"Shelley isn't here?" she said tentatively.

He led her back into the living room. "No, not for the moment." Biggy began the build-up. "I think he's over at one of the embassies. Belgian or something. The ambassador's wife is trying to haggle over the price of a painting she's been wanting to buy for months."

"Oh." Connie frowned at him and then she, too, understood who the other must be. "Why, you're Mr. Warren."

"Biggy," he said. "Shell's one of my best friends." His smile turned wry. "Sometimes I think my only one. Sit down, Connie. We'll wait for him. Did Shell tell you I was staying here?"

"Why yes, he did." Connie settled down on the couch, after depositing her packages on one of the chairs. She was mildly disappointed at Shelley not being home. She'd wanted to show him what she'd bought on her shopping tour. Prices in Paris were considerably lower than she had expected and with the twenty per cent discount given if you bought with American travelers' checks, she'd outdone herself.

She looked at the cartoonist. Bigelow Warren, at first glance, didn't suggest the sharp-witted creator of a youthful cynic like *Bobby*. He looked too … well … gentle of character, too easygoing, albeit somewhat sad behind his good nature. Bigelow didn't know it, but he had a surpassing charm for women. He so obviously needed a woman, needed to be taken care of, even babied. Big as he was, he gave the impression of a neglected child. There was a woebegone something about the shaggy cartoonist.

"How about a drink, Connie?" Bigelow suggested. "Shell has quite a selection here."

"A coke, maybe. I had enough last night to last me for a while." She grinned ruefully and in self-deprecation. "I'm afraid I'm not much of a drinking girl."

He went over to the sideboard, got out a tall glass, a bottle of the soft drink and some ice from the thermos container. "That's a relief, for a change," he said over his shoulder. He poured her drink, then stared for a long moment at the array of bottles before sighing and taking a coke for himself.

He brought the drinks back and took a chair across from her. He toasted her. "Well, here's to you and Shell."

She lifted her glass in response, then touched it to her lips. "You know," she said, "this is my opportunity to check up on that laddybuck of mine. He said you were his best friend."

The big cartoonist shifted in his chair. He supposed that was right. Shell didn't have much in the way of real friends. The poor guy, in spite of his hedonistic way of life, was going through a tough period and Biggy knew it. However, the answer, if there was one, had to be in Shell's own efforts, it couldn't come from outside.

"Yep," Bigelow said. "We've been buddies for the past several years. The first person I look up whenever I get to Paris is Shell."

She leaned forward. "Do you really think he's a *great* artist, Mr. Warren?"

He shook his head. "Nope. And you should never ask that question of one artist about another. Every artist thinks everyone else's work is sheer tripe. And call me either Bigelow, or, better still, Biggy."

She laughed easily. She liked this big shaggy friend of Shelley's. He had a comfortable ease about him.

"Hmmm," she said accusingly. "I'm a great admirer of *Bobby*, but you don't really think of cartooning as Art, do you?"

"Yep," he said definitely. "There is Art and art, of course, but I've often wondered why people think that visual art must be in oil before it can be a masterpiece. Why can't it be a sketch, a watercolor—even, possibly, a cartoon? Why, when people think of great literature, does it have to be a novel, or, if poetry, an epic? Why not a short story, or a simple half-dozen-line verse?"

She took another sip of the drink she didn't really want and put the glass down on the cocktail table. She frowned for a moment, staring down at the tip of her shoe, before saying suddenly, "Bigelow, Shelley's changed a lot."

He shifted uncomfortably again. Confound it, he liked this girl and consequently *didn't* like the position he found himself in. He had thought it would be fun, and nobody hurt, but it wasn't proving out. Bigelow Warren wasn't by nature a liar, and this was possibly beyond the limits of a joke.

He said slowly, "Connie, everybody changes. The Shell you see here in Paris isn't the college boy you knew back in Ohio—and never will be again. We haven't known each other long enough for me to be giving you advice, however, I might suggest that you make haste with care. Be sure you know this new Shell, that you're not confusing him with the old."

She forced a laugh. "My. You don't sound like the humorist you're cracked up to be, Bigelow. Either that, or you're trying to gently break the news that Shelley has taken up smoking opium."

He grinned wryly. "It goes both ways, of course. Possibly you've changed a great deal, too, in four or five years."

She was thoughtful. "Maybe we shouldn't have allowed ourselves to be separated for so long. I *do* feel Shelley is different. And perhaps you're right, perhaps he feels the same about me."

"I feel like a wet blanket," Biggy rumbled, "and you're probably all keyed up with your first visit to Paris." He looked at his watch. "See here, it's time to eat and Shell isn't back yet. Let's leave a note for him and take off for some three-star restaurant, say the Tour d'Argent. You're the first real, alive, healthy American girl without a thick coating of phony sophistication I've run into in a coon's age and I'd like to take advantage of your company. You'd be surprised at the humbug glitter they all manage to put on in New York and here in Paris."

"What!" she wailed. *"Real, healthy American girl?* And me spending long hours of torture and scads of money in the best beauty shops in Cincinnati to acquire my sophisticated look."

He laughed, then drawled, "Yep. You might work away at looking like Marlene Dietrich, but beneath it all, little gal, yore just my Sally from down in the Ozarks."

She looked at her watch. "Ha," she said. "You're probably right, though. It looks as if Shelley is being held up. All right, the Tour d'Argent it is." She imitated his drawl. "Let's see if they can do up this little Ohio farm girl some corn bread, succotash and kanip."

Biggy closed his eyes and shuddered. "Claude Terrail and his staff pride themselves on being able to please the tastes of every gourmet who ever enters the Tour d'Argent. It's one of the best three or four restaurants in the world. What in the world is kanip?"

Connie said spritely, "In Philadelphia they call it scrapple. If this here city slicker, Claude Terrail, doesn't know how to make kanip I'll give him my recipe. You cook the meat offen the head of a hog, comes butchering time, and you mix it with corn-meal mush, Then you take—"

"Come on, come on," Bigelow moaned in mock anguished surrender.

"I'll hafta go to my room and get my Sunday, go-to-church bonnet," Connie told him primly. "It ain't often I git to eat store-boughten vittles."

"Everybody tries to get into the act," the cartoonist moaned. "Who's the humorist around here, anyway?"

She stood up, preparatory to going to her own room for her things. "I'll be good," she said.

Bigelow looked at her in honest appreciation. Offhand, he couldn't remember ever taking to a girl so quickly. There seemed, even after this short half-hour or so of company, to be a ... well, almost intimate relationship between them.

He scowled at her, grinning at the same time. "There's no chance we've met somewhere before, is there?"

"Nope," she said over her shoulder, on the way to the door. She smiled at him. "Worse luck. I like you, Biggy."

* * * *

Shell was having no difficulty finding guests for the party. The habitués of the Left Bank seldom have opportunity to loll in such luxury as the Geroge Fifth provided.

But Shell was being selective. He wanted his artists to look like artists, his poets to sound like poets—seemingly normal characteristics usually lacking. He wanted his titled refugees not only to look the part but dress it, and that was often a snag. Most of the Left Bank aristocracy had long since hocked or sold their finery and uniforms, not to speak of the family jewels.

He dealt only with those he knew he could trust, and gave each a quick rundown on the situation. He was giving a party for a girl from the States. He wanted to impress her. Lay it on thick.

They understood. They were of a class that had done the equivalent before—and often—and for less value received than this promised evening of top food and drink in the company of their fellows.

By the time he checked his watch, it was getting late. Connie would be back at the hotel. He phoned her room and got no answer. He phoned Bigelow Warren's suite and got no answer there, either. He phoned the *concierge* and was informed that Mr. Warren and Miss Lockwood had left the hotel after requesting that he, the *concierge*, make reservations for them at the Tour d'Argent.

Well, that was all right. The night before had been a drain on Shell's meager resources and he couldn't afford to take Connie to another expensive restaurant. And he certainly didn't mind her being in Biggy's company. He rather liked the idea of the cartoonist and Connie getting to know each other. His girl and his best friend.

He had about decided to return to the George Fifth for something to eat—he could put his meal on the tab—but he decided that since he'd been dashing around like crazy all day, he could use an *apéritif* at the Deux Magots.

By luck his favorite table was empty, a rare occasion these days, especially now that the tourist season had fully opened up. He called for Maurice to bring him a Berger.

Sissy Patterson came striding by—for once without Mike Brett-James—clutching a piece of paper in one hand. She looked as though she had something worrisome on her mind.

The sight of her drove all thoughts of Connie, the party, Biggy and the guests from his mind. He realized suddenly and definitely that he'd never met a woman so capable of *projecting* her personality upon him. There was something she had for him—possibly for him alone, he didn't know—that other women simply hadn't and could never have. It wasn't just the rapport they found physically. No, not just that.

Hold it, Shell Halliday, he told himself. *The bridges have been burned. She isn't for you. You're already up to your neck in complications. And even if there was no Connie, Sissy isn't for you. Play it light and flippant, Shell Halliday, that's what she expects.*

"Hi, there," he called, waving nonchalantly.

She came over. "Shell," she exclaimed. "You're just the one I need."

He got to his feet, held a chair for her. "That has a sinister ring to it," he said. "Who do you need worked over?"

"Worse than that," she said.

"Great. Have a drink. On me, for a change."

"No time. We can have one over there. She probably has a bar. We have to hurry. It's getting dark and the lights are out."

He looked at her sadly. "Poor thing. You've obviously slipped your clutch."

"Good Heavens," she said, "do come alive, Shell. I don't know anything about Paris and I've got to find this address." She handed the paper to him.

He looked at it. "Rue de la Colombe. Sure, it's over on the Ile de La Cité, near Notre Dame. Little street, only about a block long. Has a cute little restaurant on it, the La Colombe, where Bemelman hangs out a lot. Nice place."

"Well, hail a cab or something and take me there."

Shell shrugged, escorted her to the curb and began searching the traffic stream for a taxi. "Do you mind telling me why?"

"Oh, a supposed friend of mine, a nasty witch who's always talking behind my back, has a studio there. Wants me to check it for her. I made the mistake of sending her a post card and when she found out I was in Paris she gave me this chore to take care of."

A cab swerved in, almost banging the curb. Another Parisian cowboy behind the wheel, Shell thought grimly. He held the door open for Sissy, climbed in after her, and hardly had time to get the door closed before they ripped back into the traffic. The driver's head turned completely away from the street ahead and he looked questioningly at Shell, ignoring cars, trucks and pedestrians.

"A la Rue de la Colambe!" Shell said in hurried anguish. *"Et regardez la circulation, s'il vous plaît."*

The driver made with a Gallic shrug. *"Très bien, très bien, Monsieur."*

Shell looked back at Sissy. "What chore?"

"Oh, she leased the place and the tenant has evidently taken off somewhere or other and Maggie is afraid he might have lifted some of her treasures." She fished a letter from her purse. "She wants me to check on a Modigliani painting, whatever that is."

Shell pursed his mouth. "If she has a Modigliani, it's worth swiping."

"And she has some ceramic things, and some pre-Colombian statuary from Central America."

They slammed down St. Germain to Rue Dante, swung left across traffic, miraculously getting through, and crossed the Seine on the Pont au Double. Notre Dame Cathedral was immediately to their right. The cab began twisting and turning down tiny side streets.

"Good Heavens, she wouldn't have a studio in a part of town like this. Maggie is a terrible snob," Sissy mused.

"It's the latest thing," Shell told her. "Rent a rundown hole in some horrible side street, then spend a fortune fixing it up inside. Cost you more before you're through than getting a place in a good Right Bank neighborhood."

The cab drew up in a squealing of brakes and the driver turned and beamed on Shell. *See!* he seemed to be saying, *We've made it safely.*

While Sissy paid the taxi off, Shell spent a few moments ferreting out the address. It turned out to be a stairway, leading shakily up into darkness. Shell went first, just for luck.

"You have a key?" he called back to her.

"Yes, she mailed me a spare. She said I could stay here for the balance of my Paris sojourn if I wanted." Sissy grunted something Shell couldn't make out, other than that it ended in *Good Heavens.*

They reached a door in a dimly lit hall and she gave him the key. He fumbled at the lock. "This probably has to be it," he growled. "The stairs seem to go up another flight, but they look blocked off. What a joint. I wouldn't be surprised to see a placard reading *François Villon Slept Here.*"

"Who was he?" Sissy said. "Something like a French George Washington?"

The door swung open. "Not exactly," Shell said. "He was more like me—a bum and free-loader."

Before entering the studio apartment, she shot a glance at him. "Stop beating yourself," she said. "You're not as bad an egg as you seem to think you are."

"If I knew how to curtsy, I would," Shell said sourly. "However, this particular egg shouldn't be served to a Chinaman."

They were in the studio apartment. Shell had been correct. Rent on this building was probably infinitesimal, but the owner had lavished a small fortune on the interior-decorating, upon the furniture and art objects it contained.

"I don't get the connection," Sissy said. "Good Heavens, Maggie certainly did herself proud here. Look at that Javanese, or whatever it is, bar."

Shell was standing before the fireplace, staring up at the startling Modigliani above it. "What connection?" he said. Then he went on to comment, "Indonesian, and it's made of carved teak but otherwise is a phony. Indonesians are mostly Moslem."

"What's serving bad eggs got to do with Chinamen?" She looked at him critically. "And what's the fact that Indonesians are Moslems got to do with the bar being phony?"

He said in explanation, "It was supposed to be funny, but it didn't come off. Chinese are supposed to eat hundred-year-old eggs as a delicacy. How bad could an egg get? Moslems don't drink, so they don't make bars. This one was probably made here in Paris to your friend's order. No wonder she wanted you to check. That painting's worth at least twenty-five thousand."

Sissy said, "Let's start all over again. We're talking about at least three different things at once." She stared up at the painting. *"That's* worth twenty-five thousand dollars? Why—" She came over and stood beside him, and put her hands on her hips. "—she looks as though she's got three breasts."

Her stance had emphasized her own magnificent breasts and, inadvertently, Shell's eyes went down to them.

His mouth seemed suddenly to go dry.

He collected himself and redirected his gaze, meeting her eyes. They were open, clear, bright and gold-flecked. But Sissy had caught his momentary arousal at the realization of her body and its nearness and the memories it brought back. Sissy Patterson possessed the most desirable body Shell had ever experienced.

Her eyes seemed to go cloudy and her usually animated face went beautifully sensuous. Her hands dropped to her sides, and she swayed a fraction of an inch toward him.

He grasped her roughly and pulled her toward him. In the back of his mind something said once, twice, *Connie,* but then it was gone, and as though from the floor, an ebbing of passion swept up and over both of them.

Her mouth went slack, as it always did in the grip of desire. She was the ideal love instrument. Played upon, she responded completely, to the utmost of her capabilities—and they were considerable.

Her tongue, undirected, darted about the inner surfaces of his lips, commanding him to readiness for her. Her breasts, nipples so hard as to be felt through her clothing and his, seemed to swell in response to his masculinity and its needs.

He stared, almost glared, into her eyes as their mouths twisted upon each other, and her own eyes narrowed, then rolled upward. Air went out of her lungs and her knees weakened and she felt close to complete faint.

They stumbled toward the studio couch, not knowing nor caring if or how they made it. Had they not made it, the floor would have done just as well.

They fumbled with buttons, zippers and belt buckle, working together, getting in each other's way in their frantic haste.

"No, it goes like this," she muttered. "Oh … quick."

There, in each of their minds, was the memory of the last time, and each knew it had been the best time. In all their two lives of sex play and passion, of casual affairs and longer affairs, in their dealings with sex-sophisticates or amateurs, with whoever—it had never been so perfect for Sissy as with Shell, never been so perfect for Shell as with Sissy.

He had never met a woman so spontaneous to arousal. Nor one who aroused him so quickly. He was already rampant.

He bent over her expertly, bit one of the cosmetic-coral tips of her full breasts, amazed that even in repose, upon her back, the perfect mounds lost none of their shape. He bit gently. Too gently. She seized his head in her hands and pressed him down on it.

"Harder," she moaned. "Bite me, Shell."

He played a few moments' homage to her breasts, knowing that she was already fully ready for him, and he for her, but prolonging it, torturing them both.

His lips circled the hard softness and he marveled at the fact that she had borne a child. Her skin was that of an untouched fourteen-year-old.

She threw her arms back over her head and closed her eyes. His face was flushed, and she could feel its heat, even as tongue and lips caressed her intimately.

She muttered in agony, "Do … do those things you did before … Shell. Oh, do everything to me. Everything you can think of."

His response was unintelligible.

* * * *

They lay nude on the studio couch and stared at each other in growing comprehension.

"Good Heavens, this is it, isn't it?" she said finally, in wonder.

He nodded. "Yeah. I guess so. Never happened to me before."

"Me either. How come we didn't know sooner?"

"I don't know. I think maybe I did. Underneath."

"Why didn't you say anything?" Her eyes were wide and wondering.

"I don't know. I couldn't figure out any way to make it go. I'm still not sure, but there must be a way." There was puzzlement in his voice.

"How to make what go?"

"You and me. A permanent deal. First, I've got to get out of this situation I'm in."

She frowned gently, her eyes still wondering.

He worried at it. "I'll have to get a job—"

"Money doesn't make—"

He interrupted her quickly. "I'm not going to be Number Three, Sissy—your third kept man."

She flushed.

"I'm going to be Number One. Your first *real* huband, and your last one. It'll take more time, but that's the way it's got to be."

"Yes," she said softly. "Of course."

Connie came back to him, and he wondered about her fear of pregnancy. He closed his eyes in mental anguish. "I've got some things I have to work out, Sissy."

She smiled at him lazily, the after effects of their exertions making her sleepy now.

"They'll take some time," he said unhappily. Connie couldn't really be pregnant. He was sure she couldn't. Possibly he could go through the motions though, go through an act with her. Pretend to make the engagement, to ease her mind, then, when she found out it was a false alarm, he could, by mail, break the engagement.

But suppose she *was* pregnant? It was unlikely but, nevertheless, it was possible. Damnably possible.

"You'll have to bear with me, Sissy. Somehow, I'll work it out. We're a team, you and me—Sissy and Shell, and that's the way it's going to have to be. Forget about this Mike Brett-James—"

"Already have," she murmured sleepily.

"—and bear with me for just a while."

CHAPTER 7

THE PARTY got off to a bang of a start. The physical elements, of course, were impeccable. The junior chef who presided in the kitchen was supplemented by a bartender and a waiter. The hors d'oeuvres were unending and superb. Bigelow Warren was capable of going as overboard on his food as on his drink and his conception of tidbits at a party went far and beyond the usual caviar, cheese-dips and stamp-sized sandwiches. In fact, he leaned heavily on such items as Swedish *sil*, poached oysters, *paprika beif-nets*, lobster *barquettes*, and miniature *shish kebabs* served Indo-Chinese style in a peanut sauce. And he kept it coming. Champagne was the order of the day, but anything else, anything at all, was immediately at hand. Biggy was going to make Connie's party a success if anything he could do, including expenditure of any amount, could make it so.

For the first couple of hours, and while the guests were still dribbling in, Gordon Payant occupied a corner with his guitar, seemingly oblivious to the group gathered around him. He strummed softly, sang largely Mexican *mariacha* pieces. His little club didn't open until later, and he was able to put in an hour or so for Shell. Connie had been impressed; she had once seen the Negro folk singer in a minor part he'd played in a British film.

Inviting Dave Shepherd had been an inspiration. The effeminate, gushing expatriate had taken over the task of impressing Connie with the names of those present. Snob though he was, it never occurred to Dave to mention the fact that the Grand Duke Manfred was currently a waiter. Instead, he bent Connies's ear for ten minutes describing how the man's title went back to the Holy Roman Empire.

Dave, in fact, was one of the few guests who hadn't been let in on the secret of the party. He was safe. Town crier he might be, and the most insidious tattle in Paris, but he never did his gossiping on the spot. In any gathering, Dave Shepherd enthusiastically gushed over and about everyone present. The next day would be different and the bouncing extrovert could be depended upon to tell anyone within earshot about how Bigelow Warren's party was overflowing with has-beens or never-weres.

But now he was in his glory. "My dear," he whispered to Connie, "you absolutely must get to *know* this couple who just came in."

"Oh?" Connie said. She was somewhat impressed by Dave's hushed voice, but was beginning to weary of the fluttery man's company. "Who are they?"

"Well now, my dear, *he* is the Viscount Brett-James and, oh, ever so many other titles. The Brett-James family, of course, you've read about." He giggled deprecation. "*Anyone* who has ever read *any* history of England…"

"Of course," Connie said vaguely.

"Back to William the Conqueror. Oh, so many dukes and princes, earls and viscounts in the family tree. Ever so many. Scads."

"Who's she?" Connie asked interestedly. Sissy Patterson, who had a tendency toward shyness in new waters, particularly if she hadn't had a few drinks, was, in a way, conspicuous in this company—by her lack of conspicuousness. She looked what she was; a friendly, open American girl.

"The girl with Michael?" Dave Shepherd said. "Well now, my dear, I understand she is one of the *Florida* Pattersons, you know. Just *piles* of money. You know the type."

"I'll have to go over and meet them," Connie said, by way of escaping him.

Shell had been deep in an argument with Jan Luchtvaart over Utrillo's Montparnasse scenes. The Dutch painter, as usual, was in corduroys and wore, even here at the party, a velvet beret. Shell wonderd vaguely how he'd ever got past Nicolas, down at the door. The rest of the guests were in their finery, ranging from the near-shabby to the fantastic dress uniform of the Grand Duke Manfred von Nauheim und zur Lüneburg. Shell himself couldn't help but be impressed. Most of the evening wear, he realized, was probably rented, but you had to give this gang credit; has-beens and international bums they might be, but the greater percentage of them had, in their time, been on the top one way or the other and they knew the graces and amenities.

To see the grand duke help pass a tray of Celery Victor to former Prima Donna Carla Pezzoli, it would never have occurred to anyone that this same day he very possibly had brought the aging voice teacher her morning wallop of cognac at the Flore café, which was immediately around the corner from the third floor music studio in which she attempted to make a living.

Shell saw Sissy and Mike Brett-James at the door, excused himself to Jan Luchtvaart, and made his way toward them, patting a back here, urging food and drink on the guests there, as he progressed. Thus far it was a great party.

"Sissy!" he greeted her. He turned to her companion, who seemed to be riding his high horse tonight. "Hello, Mike, welcome to the party. Let me take your things." He called to the waiter, supplied by the George Fifth, "Here, Félix, put these in the other room."

He was trying to play it smooth but inwardly Shell Halliday was churning. He hadn't expected Sissy to attend the party. He'd made a point of *not* notifying her of the date. He had a desperate feeling of things closing in; it had been complicated enough before, but this was chaos. He was playing with too many cards in his hand, and the Gods held the joker.

He had planned—how confused can you get?—to go through with his farce with Connie. Announce the engagement, and then hustle her back to the States as per Biggy's scheme. Once home again, she would be under control—if only, please God, she wasn't pregnant—and the fake engagement could be broken in as gentle a manner as possible. Meanwhile, he would be laying the foundations for his new life with Sissy.

It was complicated, *too* complicated, but it might have worked, except that Sissy was now on the scene !

She handed over her bag as well as her coat and grinned at him. "Looks like we're late, Shell. In fact, we're lucky we made it at all. Somebody fouled up on the invitations and it was just sheer luck we heard a couple of the guests talking about the party at the Deux Magots."

Was she teasing him? Shell didn't know. When they'd invited her to the party, the other night at Harry's, she'd been told only that it was for an old girl friend of Shell's from Ohio. Now, perhaps, in view of their newly discovered relationship, she'd be amused to see him with an old girl friend.

Shell muttered something, which probably didn't make sense, and tried to get control of his thinking. He *had* to come up with something.

Mike looked about the room, taken aback. "This is your suite, Halliady?" The Britisher seemed to have a thick enough hide, he showed no embarrassment before Shell over their men's-room altercation.

Shell said evenly, "It belongs to the George Fifth, but I'm temporarily occupying it."

Connie had come up, smiling, and Shell took a deep breath and said, "Connie, let me present you to two of my more recent ... friends. Felicity Patterson and Michael Brett-James." He tried to lighten things. "Mike is one of those stuffy Englishmen you always see portrayed in the movies, Connie."

"Oh, I say," Mike protested stuffily.

Connie laughed and shook hands. "I never expected Shell to meet so many people," she said. "You'll have to forgive me if I don't remember your names right away. Let's see now, Felicity and Mike."

Mike Brett-James winced at the Americanism, but Sissy smiled openly. "Oh, you'll remember me," she said. "I'm the only honest one here ..."

Shell darted a startled look at her.

"... all the rest are foreigners, or artists, or something," Sissy concluded.

Connie laughed and said to Mike, "Did anybody ever tell you that you look like David Niven?" she said.

Mike was obviously flustered. "Like who?"

"David Niven, the movie star."

Mike was blank. "I don't believe I know any of the cinema chaps," he said.

Sissy laughed. "Good Heavens, look pleased, Mike. That was a compliment. Niven will probably sue her."

Shell had been glancing back and forth at Sissy and Connie. What he'd have to do, someway, somehow, would be to get Sissy out of the place before making the announcement. He'd simply have to figure someway of getting her to go home.

Oh Lord, Biggy was bearing down on them. To Shell, it had become increasingly obvious that the big man had developed a crush on Connie, continually eyeing her like a love-lorn giant panda.

Bigelow Warren came up, two glasses in hand. "Champagne anybody, everybody?"

Mike and Sissy both took glasses.

Sissy said, after a preliminary sip, "What is it Buchwald says? 'I like champagne because it tastes like my foot has gone to sleep.'"

Biggy was keeping himself remarkably sober, much to his own surprise. He didn't particularly know why. It was just working out that way. In the back of his mind, he was worrying about Connie and Shell—and particularly Connie, by this stage, had he known it. There should be *something* he could do to bring a fairy-story ending to this, a happy ending involving a return to Ohio, perhaps, and a cozy cottage where Connie and Shell could live ever after and Bigelow could go and visit from time to time, bringing presents to the kids and being called Uncle Biggy—

He tried to give it the light touch, saying to Sissy, "Somewhere, I've seen you before."

"Hmmm. So you don't remember. I'll give you a hint. You said I had, and I quote, 'a lotta figure'." She looked down at her Dior-sheathed figure, then up at Connie and raised her eyebrows.

Connie laughed. She liked this girl. "Some nerve," she said.

Félix came up with a tray of *petits chaussons d'anchois* and served the newcomers, and Shell excused himself to check on the other guests. Actually, he wanted a breather in which to think.

Sissy looked after him, her eyes strange. She said to Connie, "A very nice guy."

Connie cocked her head infinitesimally to the side, as though catching something unexpected. She said evenly, "Yes. Yes, he is."

Biggy said, "So am I, girls. How about another drink?"

"Good Heavens, yes," Sissy said. "We're way behind. Biggy, do you remember where we met?"

He closed one eye and squinted at her with the other. "Nope."

"In the basement of Harry's Bar. You looked like a drunken grizzly bear."

He raised an arm as though to defend himself, but said manfully, "It wouldn't have been me. I never touch the stuff."

"Come to think of it, it couldn't have been me, either," Sissy said. "I never go into bars. It isn't ladylike."

Biggy shook his head and finished the old wheeze. "Must have been two other people."

Mike was looking back and forth at them, uncomprehending.

"Where's that other drink you were promising?" she asked.

Bigelow bowed sweepingly, "Madam, right this way. Whilst Connie greets the new guests I shall do you the honors."

Mike was descended upon by Dave Shepherd who flowed over him so gushingly that the Englshman was unable to escape. Sissy winked at her escort and went off with Bigelow who got a fresh bottle of wine from the bartender, along with two glasses, and they exchanged amusing banter to one side of the room while they had a drink.

She dropped it suddenly and said, her voice even, "Shell planned to marry that girl, didn't he?"

"How did you know?" the big cartoonist asked uneasily.

There was a sudden chunk of ice in her stomach. She fought for control. "They're going to announce their engagement tonight?"

"It was supposed to be a secret."

But this couldn't be right. *It couldn't be.* When she'd asked the question, she'd thought that Connie was an *old* flame, that Shell had planned to marry her in the old days—possibly back in Ohio. But now now. Not any more. Not *her* Shell.

She held out her glass shakily for more wine. "She's … she's the girl from back home? The girl from Ohio?"

"That's right." He sensed something wrong, but couldn't put his finger on it.

Her eyes went around the room vaguely, and for a moment Biggy wondered if she was already stoned. But she said, her voice empty, "This is your suite, isn't it?"

"I'm staying with Shell. The suite's in his name, not mine," Bigelow said truthfully.

She looked at him appraisingly. "But you're paying the bills. Shell couldn't afford to rent a closet in this hotel."

He felt obligated to defend his friend and said sourly, "Shell's having a hard time, right now. I'm sorry as hell for him. There doesn't seem to be an immediate answer."

She looked out over the party, the drinking, chattering, shrilling, occasional laughter, to where Connie stood talking to an existentionalist philosopher whose sweeping air of erudition camouflaged the fact that he was supported by two streetwalkers.

"I wonder if it shouldn't be Miss Lockwood that we're sorry for," Sissy said.

Bigelow ran his ham of a hand back through his already rumpled hair. "Both of them," he said unhappily. "Both of them. Here, have some more champagne."

"Twisted my arm," Sissy said, presenting her glass. The sparkling wine was beginning to take effect and she wanted still more. She didn't want to think. She couldn't allow herself to think.

Bigelow let his eyes go around the room to check developments and just in time. "I'd better get back to the guests," he told Sissy. "The grand duke is getting to the point where he usually wants to toast the emperor and then break the glasses by tossing them into the fireplace."

"That I'd like to see," Sissy said, fighting to keep it light.

"Only there's no fireplace," Biggy growled. "See you later."

* * * *

Mike Brett-James finally shook Dave Shepherd by pleading a necessity to visit the bathroom.

The bath lay beyond the room in which Félix had left the guests' wraps. Mike closed the bedroom door behind him and started toward the bathroom. He hesitated.

On the bed lay Sissy's conspicuously expensive evening wrap, with bag to match. Mike Brett-James darted a look back at the door through which he had just come. For a moment or so, surely, nobody would be coming through. When he'd entered this room, he hadn't noticed anyone heading in this direction.

He took a quick step to the bed, took up the bag, unsnapped it and brought forth an untidy roll of various currencies—francs dollars, pounds and pesetas. He returned the bag to its former position on the bed and went on to the bath.

* * * *

The party was well on its way. Under the influence of food and drink in monstrous quantities, the guests were unlimbering, each in his individual way. The two models, respectively redhead and brunette, who had got into the quarrel about their chest measurements and wanted to demonstrate, were talked into taking a tape measure and going off on their own into one of the baths to procure the evidence. Carla Pezzoli, who had got away with enough Mumm's Cordon Rosé to float a small yacht, was moved to tears over her past glories at La Scala. Shell led her off to the small balcony where he got her seated with an ice bucket and a fresh bottle, and listened for a few moments to her opinion that Callas knew a *bank* note better than a *musical* one.

He got back inside and took a deep breath. He had to talk to both Biggy and Sissy. Somehow he had to head off disaster. He spotted Biggy in a group and headed over in that direction.

The big cartoonist was telling one of his jokes.

"So this American private—just landed in Laos, see—comes up to the captain and says, 'Sir, there's just one thing that bothers me. How do I tell the difference between a Laotian on our side and one on the Pathet Lao's? They all look the same to me and I'm afraid I'll shoot the wrong one.' 'Well,' the captain says, 'it's simple. Suppose you're walking along a jungle path and you come face to face with a Laotian and you don't know what kind he is. You up with your gun and say, "Khrushchev is a sonovabitch," and then, according to how he reacts, you'll know whether or not to shoot.' So the private goes off and the next day the captain is walking through one of the field hopitals and there's this private stretched out on a cot all bandaged up to hell-and-gone and taking plasma and everything. So the captain says, 'Good grief, man, what happened?' And the private says, 'Well, sir, it's because of that advice you gave me. Just like you said, I was walking along this jungle path and all of a sudden I was confronted by this Laotian and I didn't know if he was one of ours or a Pathet Lao, so I upped with my gun and I said, "Khrushchev is a sonovabitch," and he upped with his gun and said, "Kennedy is a sonovabitch," and while we were shaking hands on it, a Jeep came along and hit both of us.'"

While most of them were laughing, one Shell knew as a former foreign correspondent now turned expatriate alcoholic, said, "You can't say things like that."

Biggy looked at him quizzically. "Why not?"

"Why, damn it, you just can't. No American is going to put up with that kind of story. It's not funny."

Bigelow said gently, "You're out of time, Steve. Humor goes in cycles. Back in the Twenties and Thirties old Will Rogers made himself the humorist of his time with gags based on political connotations. Twenty years later, in the McCarthy era, it was bad taste, if not outright dangerous, to say practically anything amusing about political policies and top politicians. Now the pendulum is swinging again. That's why guys like Mort Sahl become so popular. That's why my *Bobby* strip has made a hit."

"Never liked it myself," Steve grunted. "Surprised you aren't investigated by the Un-American Activities Committee."

Biggy shrugged hugely. "You've been out of the country too long, Steve. Time marches on. Did it ever occur to you that when a country gets to the point where you can't make cracks about the politicians, it's lost an element of democracy?"

Shell moved in, looking at Bigelow worriedly. The burly cartoonist didn't seem to be drunk, but all they needed was for him to get into one of his hassles.

He muttered into the big man's ear, "Hey, pal, save it for the next *Bobby* strip. Let's not go annoying the guests."

Biggy grinned at him. "I'm okay, Shell. In fact, the way I feel, I'm beginning to suspect I'm over my toot. I think I'll probably be going back to the States in a few days. By the way, that Connie is one fine girl. I think you're crazy not to go on back to Ohio and marry her before it's too late."

Even as he was talking, Shell grew wearily impatient of the words. The thing had got far and beyond the complications Biggy knew about. Shell's eyes went around the room while he waited for his friend to come to the end of his point. He was going to have to tell the other about Sissy.

His supposed friends were all well along by now—the supposed artists, the supposed titled aristocrats, the supposed writers and celebrities. Actually, Bigelow was the only real success in the place. The next nearest thing to it were the three servants; the junior chef, bartender and waiter. At least, they'd worked their way into good jobs in their chosen fields. All the rest present, including himself, were failures.

Something suddenly came to him.

Some of these has-beens and never-weres were not above picking up a dishonest buck, given the opportunity. And if he knew Sissy, she'd presented an open opportunity to all. She was dressed obviously in the top products of Parisian *haute couture*, which would tip off anyone to the fact that there was probably folding money in her bag. And now that he recalled, her bag had gone into the bedroom to be deposited on an easily available bed.

He knew the George Fifth servants were above supicion, but except for Connie, Biggy, Brett-James and possibly Dave Shepherd, nobody else present was a certainty.

"Look, Biggy," Shell said. "That's what I wanted to talk to you about. This engagement announcement. I'll be back in just a minute." He headed for the bedroom.

He wasn't sure just which one was hers and stood for a few moments, staring down at the coats, bags and hats which were strewn on the bed. He vaguely remembered handing her things to Félix. What was it she had worn? Oh, yes. It came back to him. Here was the coat, and here the matching bag. He picked it up and looked about the room. It shouldn't be too much of a problem to find a safe place. He could put it into a bureau drawer and get it for her when she was about to leave. He could lock the drawer and keep the key.

Bag in hand, he started toward the bureau. There was quite a bit of noise going on in the living room. He'd better hurry this up and get back to Biggy and—

The bedroom door opened and Sissy came in, her face empty, wan beneath her make-up. She closed the door behind her, blocking out the jabber and laughter of the other room.

"Shell," she said in a strange voice, "up to the last minute I thought you'd have some sort of an explanation for me. But, Shell, your friend Biggy just announced your engagement to … to that girl."

"Holy Smokes," Shell groaned. "Listen, Sissy,—"

Her eyes went to the bag in his hand and she frowned, uncomprehending, and then, unbelievingly.

"Shell," she said. "What do you have there?"

He began to say something, stumbled. How could he tell her that all these people, his supposed friends, were such that he couldn't trust them not to pilfer her belongings?

She took the bag from him, still frowning uncomprehendingly, and opened it. She looked into it for a long moment and then there was a slump to her shoulders.

She said, very softly, "You might have at least left me taxi fare, Shell."

Suddenly, protecting the good names of his supposed friends was meaningless. "Look, Sissy," he began with a rush, "I had just picked it up—"

"Never mind," she said bluntly, refusing to hear his protests. "It doesn't make any difference. It's only money. Only money. Good night, Shell. Mike and I will be leaving. Good luck with Connie." She hesitated before adding, cruelly, "She'll need it."

"Sissy! Damn it, listen to me!"

She looked full into his face. "Why?" she said bluntly.

She grabbed up her coat and was gone.

He stood, gaping after her. What was there he could do to prove his innocence, to prove that the evidence was circumstantial? Go out and demand that all the guests allow themselves to be searched? For that matter, two or three had already left, pleading other engagements. Some had actually had to go to work in night spots or less reputable establishments.

He followed her into the living room.

Sissy was atop a chair, a glass of champagne in her hand, and was shouting for attention.

Attention was difficult to obtain. The servants were bustling about, pouring fresh wine, and the guests were largely clustered around Connie, who stood next to Biggy accepting the congratulations of all. There was a strangely peaked expression on her face, almost as though this wasn't necessarily the happiest moment of her life.

"Hey, everybody," Sissy shrilled. "Hey, me, too!"

Heads turned to her.

"Me and Mike. We announce our engagement, too."

Mike had come toward her when she had first climbed up on the chair. Now he looked up at her flushed face.

"Oh now, really, my dear," he said. "Really, you know. A more propitious occasion and all that. Possibly back in London."

Sissy looked down at him. "Mike," she said, "you're an old stuffed shirt, but I'll marry you anyway. Catch!" She dribbled some of her champagne over his head.

While the room laughed, Mike shambled backward hurriedly, out of range, grabbing his handkerchief from his breast pocket and dabbing awkwardly.

"Oh, I say," he protested.

Some of the guests spotted Shell emerging from the bedroom and crowded in on him, making it momentarily impossible for him to get through. Other elements in the party had closed around Connie, Sissy and Brett-James as they moved across the room, saying their good-byes as they went.

In sheer mental agony, Shell Halliday could see Sissy at the door, about to leave.

He could have pushed through. He could have made some scene. But to what end?

Could she have possibly believed him? Hardly. Sissy Patterson had had her disappointments in men before. Now she expected them. It was nothing new to have her husband or lover turn out to be interested in her money, rather than Sissy herself.

He felt queerly empty. For the first time in days, his mind wasn't churning in the attempt to bring up some all-encompassing answer to all the fouled-up imbroglio that confronted him. He had given it up.

In the hallway of the George Fifth, Sissy and Brett-James made their way toward the elevator, Sissy marching very erect, Mike trailing in puzzled fashion, slightly to the rear. The glow of champagne was completely gone from her now, and she was infinitely weary. However, Mike was still in the spirit of the party—to the extent that Mike Brett-James was ever capable of entering into the spirit of a party.

"I say, my dear," he said. "Why are we dashing off so precipitately? I was just beginning to enjoy myself. Some of those chaps are quite clever, you know. And that tipping the champagne over my head—I'm not angry, you know—but it was a bit of a rag, what?"

"I'm sure," Sissy said bitterly. "However, I hope you have cab fare, darling. It seems our host just ransacked my pocketbook with disastrous results."

The Britisher stiffened. "I say," he said.

Sissy went on, still bitterly, "I shouldn't have said that. I knew what Shell was and could have stayed away from him if I objected to his way of life. All right, so he ran true to form. What am I complaining about?"

"But the man should be thrashed," Mike blurted. He paused as though to turn back.

"Oh, come on, Mike," Sissy said impatiently. "That overgrown rhinoceros of a friend of his would break you in half if you caused any trouble."

"But one should do *something*. Are you sure it was Halliday?"

Sissy pressed the button for the elevator. She said wearily, "I caught him doing it—bag in hand."

Mike let air out of his lungs as though in indignation. In truth, it was in relief.

"Good Heavens, Mike," Sissy said. "I don't know what we're upset about. We should be happy. We're engaged. I've made up my mind, at last. Let's take off for London, or Scotland, or your Irish estate tomorrow. Let's cable little Bunny to join us. We'll get married immediately."

"Well, one must post the banns you know," Mike said. "But, my dear, we'll see what we can do in the way of expediting things. I have influential friends, of course."

The door of the elevator opened and two Americans emerged, talking and chuckling in alcoholic volubility.

"Good old Biggy," one of them was saying. "Brother, will he be surprised."

They were both very well lit. The second said, "Yeah, he thinks we're back slaving over his gags. This'll stop him."

Sissy pointed and said wearily, "Down that way, gentlemen. Where you hear the noise. You're just in time for the party."

The first of the two eyed her figure appreciatively. "Hey, don't go way just when we're arriving," he protested. "If there's a party, it won't be the same without you."

"Just watch your wallets," Sissy said grimly. The door closed behind her and Mike.

The one gag man said to the other, "What'd she say?"

"Damned if I know. Except Biggy is throwing a party. Let's go. The edge is beginning to wear off."

Félix answered the door, gave them one swift covering glance and opened wide. They were obviously invited guests.

The second one said, "Listen, Bill, let's not even let Biggy know we're here until he spots us. You know, we'll have a glass in one hand and something to eat in the other, and he'll come up against us, not thinking, and *bam*, it'll hit him. What're we doing here instead of back in New York?"

"Right, Sammy," said Bill. "Snag a coupla drinks off that tray. Isn't this the same suite Biggy had that time all three of us came over together?"

"Looks like it."

The two gag men, drinks in hand, filtered into the milling, hard-drinking crowd. They could see Bigelow Warren, his back to them, at the far side of the room, obviously in animated conversation.

A girl came up to them, smiling. "How did I miss meeting you?"

"Shucks," Sammy said. "How did *we* miss meeting you?"

She laughed, not quite understanding. "I'm Connie Lockwood," she said.

"And we're Bill and Sam," Bill said. He grinned. "And not *exactly* party crashers. We work for Biggy. He gets all the dough and we do all the work."

"We need a union," Sam said. "Hey, there's old Shell over there."

"You know Shell, too?" Connie said, smiling. She realized the two were already tight but, by this time, practically everybody else was, too.

"Do we know Shell? Without Shell our boss'd be a goner. Good old seeing-eye dog, Man Friday, pick-up-the-pieces Shell. The best-hearted, lousiest artist, biggest free-loader in Paris."

From across the room, Bigelow spotted them, realized with stomach-sinking horror that they were talking to Connie, and began pushing and shoving his way in their direction. No simple task in the throng.

The expression on Connies's face had dropped. She said coldly, "You're talking about your host, after all, and—"

Sam chuckled his amusement. "Host?" He picked up another champagne from the tray that sat on the table next to where they stood. "Shell couldn't afford to buy anybody a bag of peanuts. Did that tout tell a nice girl like you that Biggy's suite was his?"

Bigelow was upon them. "Hey! What are you two doing here?" He shot a quick nervous look at Connie. Her face was gray, the lipstick a slash of red on a corpse face.

"Work's all caught up, Biggy. We came over to help you celebrate. What's the occasion of the big party?"

"Our old pal, Shell," he said quickly, "is announcing his engagement to Miss Lockwood. Connie, have you met—?"

"We introduced ourselves," Connie cut in emptily. "It's true, isn't it, Mr. Warren?"

The cartoonist glared at his gag men.

Sam said blankly, "Engagement? Shell—"

"I knew it," Connie said dully. "I think that subconsciously I knew it all along. Something didn't ring true."

"Listen, Connie—"Bigelow started.

"I ... I think I'll go to my room," she said, her voice tight and hard.

"Hey, did we let something out of the bag?" Bill asked. "Why didn't somebody give us the office? We didn't—"

"Shut up," Bigelow growled at him.

* * * *

The room was a shambles. After he'd shooed out all the guests, most of them protesting, Bigelow Warren had also dismissed the help, telling them they could have the place cleaned on the following day.

Shell sat on the couch, staring emptily at the carpet, at a wet spot where somebody had spilled a nearly full glass of wine. His mind couldn't seem to function.

Bigelow, cold sober now, poured them both a stiff Scotch and added only ice cubes.

"Here," he said, proffering the other the Old-Fashioned glass.

"I don't want it," Shell said.

"Drink it anyway. You can use it."

"Yeah, okay." Shell took a breath. "Well, this tears it. The chickens are now all home to roost."

Bigelow knocked back his drink unhappily. "Maybe it's for the best, Shell." He poured himself another.

Shell looked up at the big cartoonist. "The best?" He grunted his disgust. He was going to have to tell Biggy the whole story, the whole complicated, messed-up story—but he hated to get started on it.

"You're going to have to face reality now, Shell. You've been putting it off for nearly five years. You didn't expect to spend the rest of your life here, did you?"

Shell thought about it vaguely. Biggy didn't even know about Sissy, of course. He was going to have to tell him about her.

Bigelow was saying, "You're piling it on too thick, Shell. Take your medicine. Go on back home and tell them that you've decided an artist's life isn't for you. Tell them you want to go into your Old Man's business. As for Connie ... okay, you've probably lost her but, face it, you two had drifted away from each other, anyway. She no longer meant as much to you as she had when you were both back in Ohio."

Shell ran his right hand down over his cheek, as though checking his shave, but said nothing. Bigelow was right, of course, about that part of it.

The big man went on persuasively. "Face it, Shell, she didn't. If she had, you wouldn't have brought that streetwalker up to the suite only a few days before Connie arrived."

Shell scowled at him. "Streetwalker? That's the second time you've mentioned that. What streetwalker? I never had a girl up here."

"Listen," Bigelow said impatiently, "don't kid me about it. You were passed out, but don't tell me you forgot entirely. You must have seen her again the next morning when you woke up."

Shell was staring at him, uncomprehendingly.

Bigelow chuckled. "As a matter of fact, I did your little job for you. You were out like a light."

Shell stared at him.

Bigelow chuckled again, but this time nervously. He couldn't understand Shell's expression. He said, "You were passed out here on the couch. Just as I came in—a little high myself, matter of fact—a voice called out that she was ready. So, for gags, I went in and laid her for you."

"You bastard."

Shell came slowly to his feet, his fists clenched.

"What the devil's the matter with you?" Bigelow growled. "It was just a joke."

"That was Connie," Shell said in a flat rage.

This was the root of all the trouble. This was what had fouled everything up. This had pushed him into that agreement to marriage, which had ultimately led to his disaster with Sissy. The stupid, drunken bungling of this do-gooder lush!

Within him flowered a volcanic rage such as a fundamentally easygoing nature had never revealed to him before.

Shell surged forward, sank his fist into the big man's stomach. Bigelow, overwhelmed with what the other had said as much as with the sudden attack, staggered backward, caught himself and tried to seize the younger man's arms.

"Hey, easy ..." he growled. But his heart wasn't in his defense.

Shell pulled free, lashed out again, smashing his fist into the other's nose.

Bigelow settled himself into position, pushed his left forward to Shell's shoulder, throwing the other, momentarily, off balance.

"Hold it, damnit," he growled. "Let's talk about this. I—"

Shell charged forward again, swinging freely, wildly, and landed two or three hard blows to Bigelow's face. An angry red began to show on the big man's face. He realized he would have to, inclination or no, fight this angry man who charged at him again and again, incapable of listening to reason.

A punishing blow caught Biggy in the temple and anger seeped to the surface.

"All right," he muttered, "you asked for it." But he held off, still hoping Shell's inflated anger might begin to cool.

Another of Shell's barrage of punches landed on Bigelow's nose and he felt blood spurting through one nostril. Biggy finally waded in, countering Shell's punches and offering some of his own—a drive to the chest, another to the belly, and still another to the face. Shell began to look bewildered rather than angry now that his victim had turned on him. His breath came in short gasps as he tried to find his target and found it suddenly elusive.

Bigelow, having decided that the only way the senseless fight could be stopped would be through an obvious victory on his part—and they were mismatched, there was no doubt about that, he, Biggy, had the edge in size and weight—he would have to end it quickly, painlessly—more or less.

He lunged, aiming a pile-driver blow at Shell's solar plexus and stepped on a shot glass left by some careless whiskey drinker earlier in the evening. He staggered, off balance, and felt a cruel blow at his middle, then one to his face and then his belly again. He lifted his hands to protect his face. A wild blow hit him behind the ear. Biggy's knees began to go rubbery and he sagged forward, folding like a limp doll and sinking to the floor.

CHAPTER 8

SOME TIME DURING THE NIGHT, Bigelow got up from the couch where he had crawled after Shell has stormed out of the suite. He went to the bathroom and stared into the mirror. His face wasn't as cut and bruised as he had expected it to be, but it was a mass of pain. He dabbed cold water on it, muttering to himself.

Damn and double damn.

But what use was there in taking the blame onto himself? It was no one's fault, in particular. Is anyone ever to blame when you have all the factors at hand? Poor Connie, poor Shell.

He grunted in self-pity. And poor Bigelow Warren, for that matter. He wished that Shell had cut the slaughter a little shorter. His nose felt as though a trip hammer had squashed it. He probed around in his mouth with his tongue and felt swollen, sensitive gums.

He grunted again. He could have flattened Shell, except for the unlucky shot glass. In New York, between binges, Bigelow kept himself in shape, belonged to a wrestling team at the East Side Y, and had even taken a lengthy course in judo at one time. Besides which, he must have outweighed the younger man by at least fifty pounds.

He ran a beefy paw back through his rumpled hair and made his way into the bedroom. He undressed only to the point of removing jacket, tie and shoes and then fell onto the bed and slid back into sleep.

When he awoke, it was well into the day. His face ached and he had to orientate himself, an easier task than usual since he was stone sober and without hangover. In fact, his first reaction was surprise to find himself in Paris with a clear head. Then it came back. The disastrous party. His gag men, Bill and Sammy, dropping in and spilling the beans to Connie Lockwood. Her dashing out, in tears. And then, later, his inadvertently revealing to Shell that he, Bigelow Warren, had—what would you call it?—seduced, raped his girl. Yes, by legal definition he had undoubtedly raped the girl.

Bigelow dragged himself from the bed and began shedding the clothes in which he had slept. There wasn't any way he could set things right. He knew that. But he had to start trying.

He showered hot and then cold to try to bring keenness back to his mind. He shaved carefully around still tender bruises and as he did so, gingerly ran his tongue over the sore gums. He grimaced sourly. Old Shell hadn't done as complete a job as he might have. He'd been too upset to be accurate.

The big cartoonist dressed in a dark suit, rather than the usual tweed jacket and slacks he affected in Paris. The binge was over. Somehow, deep within him, was a feeling that it was over for all time. The emotional stress of the night before had burned something out of him. He wasn't mentally organized enough, for the present, to delve further, but the feeling was there that the need for the periodic binge was gone.

He went to the phone and gave the operator Connie's room number.

Somewhat to his surprise, she answered, her voice empty.

"Connie," he said, "this is Bigelow. I'm coming around to your room. Be there in minutes."

"No—" she began to say, but he hung up.

At the door to her room, she said wearily, "I don't want to talk, Mr. Warren. Please …" She was wearing a simple translucent negligee and beneath it her nightgown.

"I do," he said. Gently, he pushed her aside, entered and closed the door behind him.

Her things littered the room. Obviously, she'd been packing.

Her eyes were dry. She had evidently got past the point of tears.

Bigelow took a chair, reversed it and sat down. He looked at her and saw what he had always seen: an inordinately attractive American Midwestern girl, unspoiled by the driving ambition that influenced most of the women he met at his work or in his social life. A girl who could probably cook and sew, who undoubtedly wanted children and to keep a home.

He wondered how many such women he had met in the past decade. Any at all?

He said abruptly, "It was my idea. It was my fault."

She sat down on the edge of the bed and said, disinterestedly, "What was your fault, Bigelow?"

At least, she'd dropped the Mr. Warren.

He summed it all up quickly. "Shell's no artist. Never was. He doesn't quite have the … the spark. But, evidently, from his early youth he was blackjacked by his parents—"

"His mother," Connie said wearily.

"—into thinking he could make a go of it in one of the toughest fields there is, legitimate art. He couldn't, Connie. Not through his own fault. However, Shell's got the sensitivity of the artist, even if he hadn't the talent it takes. He couldn't go back to … what's the name of the town?"

"New Elba," Connie said listlessly. She sat, hands in lap, almost as though she hadn't heard, and as though she was only waiting for him to finish and to leave.

"Yes, New Elba," Bigelow went on doggedly. "So for almost five years now, Shell has stayed on here in Paris making his living as best he could."

"A free-loader, a tout—those men said."

Bigelow growled something about his two gag men, then went back to his subject. "A guide is the better word. Shell beats himself in self-disgust about his way of making a living, but actually he made a point of giving service. A knowledgeable guide can make a lot of difference in a town like Paris and, in the long run, probably saves you money, even though he does get a percentage. But we're getting away from the point. The point is that when you wrote you were coming, Shell came to me in despair. I cooked up this whole scheme."

"What difference does it make?" Connie shrugged. "You were doing what you thought best, I suppose."

"This is the thing," Bigelow said pointedly. "Shell's secret has been revealed. He's no artist. Okay, but he's still Shell. Why don't the two of you go back to New Elba and start all over?"

She looked into his face and, for the first time since he had arrived, her chin trembled, and then her lips. She put her hands up suddenly to cover her face. "Do you think I haven't considered that?" She was crying.

Bigelow stood and went over to her, sat next to her on the bed and put his right arm around her shoulders. "Connie, Connie," he said. "It'll work out. Shell's a great guy, beneath everything. One of the best."

She blubbered, "But don't you understand what I'm trying to say? It's not just this. Not just that he's been lying for the past four years."

He didn't understand. "But what's the matter then? Everything's solved. You can go back to Ohio together."

"I don't love him," she wailed. "I haven't since I got here. *He's changed!"*

He stared at her. *Oh Lord, what now?*

He patted her soft shoulder awkwardly. "Well … how do you think Shell feels about you?"

"He doesn't love me any more, either. I can tell. A woman knows. He made the motions. But … oh, if I hadn't been such a fool. It's too late now."

He was bewildered again. "What's too late?"

"We *have* to get married." She turned toward him and put her arms around his neck and let herself collapse completely into tears.

"But … *why?*"

"Because I'*m going to have a baby."* Bigelow Warren wasn't the type whose mouth fell open, but now it did, wide, even as he patted her soothingly.

"A baby?" he asked foolishly.

Unashamed in her blurted confession, Connie wailed, "We slept together the other night—the night I first arrived. We both got tight and slept together and now I'm going to have a baby."

Bigelow Warren swallowed.

It was at that split moment that he realized he was in love with Constance Lockwood. Talk about being unsophisticated! Here was a girl who knew so little of the facts of life that she thought love-making inevitably led to conception—almost automatically. He'd never known anyone that naïve, and he liked it.

He swallowed again and said bluntly, determined to put her mind at ease, "Listen, Connie, you're not going to have a baby."

"Yes, I am!"

He shook his head. "No, you're not. I took ... precautions."

That was *too* much. She raised her head and shook away tears from her eyes.

He swallowed again, patted her back and kissed her forehead gently. Oh Lord, the fat was in the fire now.

He said doggedly, "Now listen a minute. It sounds impossible. Crazy. But, well, I came home that night. Shell was passed out on the couch. And ... well ... now listen, Connie, I was a bit tight too, understand? I think we were all tight ... even you."

She was wide-eyed in her incomprehension. The tears had stopped in pure amazement.

He went on painfully. "There's no use trying to fancy it up. I heard a voice say, I*'m ready, darling* and ... well ... I thought Shell had brought a ... streetwalker or somebody up to the suite. And ... well ... I thought I'd play a trick on him. The room was dark—" Bigelow swallowed again. He couldn't go any further.

As he had progressed, and the eventual truth of what he was building up to became obvious, her face had drained. She said, her voice sounding far away, as though she didn't know what she said, "I ... I thought he seemed awfully big ..."

He didn't like the way she looked, nor the way her voice sounded. She was on the verge of hysteria. This piled atop what had probably been hours of tears, anguish and worry.

"Look," Bigelow said. "Just a minute—"

He came to his feet, hurried back to his own suite and picked up the first bottle of spirits that came handy to him. He took up two glasses and hurried back to her.

She sat, as she had when he had left, on the edge of the bed, and her face was blank.

"But I ... I'm a virgin—I mean ... I was. You don't ..."

He poured a quick dollop of the liquor—it turned out to be the Metaxa—into one of the glasses. "Look, take this, Connie."

She said stiffly, "Miss Lockwood. I—"

He ignored her, forced the glass into her hand. "Toss that back. Like medicine."

He half-forced the glass to her mouth, and she obeyed him, then coughed rackingly. "What … what's that?" she sputtered.

"Brandy," he said, putting the bottle on the floor and sitting next to her again. "Now listen," he said.

"No," she shook her head violently. "I don't want to listen to you, Mr. Bigelow. I want to leave. I don't want ever to see—" Her voice was rising.

He put his hand over her mouth, as gently as possible. Her eyes popped in indignation, but before she could do anything he got out what he wanted to say.

"Listen, Connie Lockwood. I love you."

Her eyes glared for a moment, but then took on an added element of puzzlement.

He took his hand away from her mouth.

"Don't be ridiculous," she snapped.

He said doggedly, "All right, but I'm telling you. I fell in love with you that first time—well, the second time—I saw you. Just like that. The old wheeze—love at first sight, all that sort of thing. And the longer I've known you, the more it's grown. All right, now I'm going to ask you something."

"I—" she managed to croak.

"Nope. Listen to me. Up until I told you about … about the accident, you liked me, too."

Her lips tightened.

"Didn't you?"

She said nothing, tears beginning to well up in her eyes again. Not to flow, as yet, but forming. She looked miserable beyond belief.

Bigelow Warren reached down and got the bottle. This time he poured two drinks, one for her, one for himself. He put the glass into her hand.

"Drink that," he said, his voice less commanding now. "You've got to snap out of this shock you're in. You know, something like an airplane pilot after cracking up his plane."

Confound it, that wasn't the way to put it. She might misconstrue that to mean—

Bigelow went on quickly, noting that the first drink had evidently loosened her up considerably, probably due to the fact that it had been taken on an empty stomach. He doubted that she'd had breakfast. He said, "We'd built up quite a friendship, until you found out about this."

She drank the second drink, almost defiantly. She looked at him. "What difference does it make? Don't you understand? I'm … I'm ruined." Her mouth began to tremble.

"Nonsense," he snapped. "You'd think you were a Victorian. All this nonsense about becoming pregnant just because you'd been with a man once, and this idea of being ruined. You haven't had enough of a sex life, young lady. You've built up some awfully old-fashioned defenses."

Her eyes went down before his accusation.

She said, her voice low, "I'll admit I liked you … especially after I found out that Shell and I no longer had anything between us. I guess it's one of the reasons I felt so close to you the first time we met—"

She flushed. "That is, the second time we met—when we introduced ourselves."

"*You* felt that, too?" he wanted to know. Without thinking, he filled their glasses again, but while she took hers, he left his own untouched. Warren Bigelow felt no need for alcohol.

"You mean *you* did?" She was wondering.

Bigelow looked directly into her eyes. -He said, "I told you a few minutes ago, and I'm telling you again, Connie. I love you."

There's something basic about that simple statement. No pussyfooting around. It puts things on a level. It's a definite commitment.

Her eyes went down. She said, before thinking, "Well … well, if it had to happen, I'm glad it was you." Then she caught herself in horror, and her face flamed as it hadn't before.

She tried to cover with indignation. She said accusingly, as though she hadn't already mentioned the fact, "I … I was a virgin."

"I should have known," he admitted contritely. "Look, Connie, I suppose I should say I'm sorry …"

"Well, I should *think* so."

"… but I'm not."

And at that point emotions snapped and Connie Lockwood was in his arms, straining against him, her mouth on his, both of them turning off reason, muttering endearments, and working toward the fulfillment they sought.

Only one thought came momentarily to the surface in Bigelow Warren's mind and then it, too, flushed away on the tide of passion. *I can't be doing this. Not me. Because I'm impotent except when I'm drunk and with a whore.*

Her glorious breasts where in his hands and he paid suitable homage to them. Her white legs were his to touch in admiration, to stroke, to fondle. Her hips were rounded, blended into soft darknesses and then into the narrowness of her waist.

And all the pent up passion of ten years of virginity were his to reap.

They were already on the bed. They had no embarrassing distance to go. He removed the nightrobe she wore from her shoulders; the hem of her gown was so high as to make that garment meaningless.

He mounted her in love and, in full possession of all his faculties, did what he had done a few days before in drunkenness—and appreciated the difference.

There is a popular fallacy which says the human animal needs to be educated to the act of love, that the successful penetration of woman by man can be accomplished only after the study of books or the accumulation of much experience, that otherwise one or both are unsatisfied.

That morning it was proved otherwise.

She moaned in the extreme pleasure his driving maleness brought to her and her every movement was instinctively right to give all she had to give, in the deepness of her woman-body.

* * * *

He left her sleeping.

He had come to solve problems—hers and Shell's. But the problems solved were hers and his. He, Bigelow Warren. He who had never enjoyed a woman before, other than in drunken orgy, was now so deeply entwined in love that the world churned. His supposed impotence was a thing of the far, far past. He was in love. It would mean marriage, a home, kids—the works.

But there was still Shell.

Shell, who had so little in life. And here he was, Bigelow Warren, taking one of the last few possessions his friend had. His girl.

Connie had said that she and Shell had drifted apart, but did Shell feel the same way? Bigelow couldn't believe it. He was constitutionally unable to understand that any man could do less than adore Connie Lockwood, given the chance. It just didn't make sense to him that Shell would no longer want her.

Besides, hadn't Shell gone into a rage and beat him up the night before on discovering the trick the cartoonist had pulled on him and Connie? Wasn't that proof that Shell still loved the girl?

Positions were reversed. Bigelow now went out on the town, trying to locate Shell Halliday.

He phoned the Lycée Hotel on Rue Casimir DeLavigne and got old Hobbs on the line.

Shell Halliday? No, he hadn't been at the Lycée for nearly two weeks. What's more, he owed Hobbs for a week's rent. And if he knew what was good for him—

Bigelow hung up and stared at the phone thoughtfully.

So far as he knew, Shell was just about broke, and his luggage was still in Bigelow's suite. That meant he'd have a hard time getting into a hotel. Which probably meant he wasn't in a hotel. He was out on the town, somewhere.

The big cartoonist checked his watch. It was already past noon. If Shell had been drinking since the night before, he'd have a considerable edge by this time.

But where in the devil would he get the money for a binge? Drinking isn't cheap in Paris even if you stuck to *calvados*, the French applejack, or *marc*, the distilled, third or fourth squeezings of wine grapes. It wasn't cheap even if you stuck to wine, not if you were doing your drinking in bars.

Bigelow scowled in thought. Shell was probably sponging off somebody. But who? The poor guy would get himself into a frame of mind where he'd wind up jumping off the Eiffel Tower. Bigelow grunted negatively. No, he wouldn't be able to afford the elevator ride. He'd have to jump into the Seine.

At any rate, the thing to do was find him.

He kept the phone going for half an hour, ringing up those haunts where Shell was well known. It was possible that in some of the tourist bistros to which he guided the wide-eyed Bohemian-life seekers, Shell's credit was good enough to run up a bar bill.

He struck pay dirt at the Vieux Caveau. The weary clean-up man who answered the phone let him know that Shell Halliday wasn't there but he had been earlier. In fact, he was the last customer to leave. They'd had to throw him out in order to close.

Where had he gone?

Who knew? Except that, by the looks of him, he'd gone somewhere to find another drink.

Bigelow ran a hefty paw back through his tousled hair. If he couldn't solve this problem, nobody could. He'd binged around Paris enough times to have been faced with the problem of where to get a drink in the early hours when the clubs were closed down and the ordinary bars not usually opened as yet.

He got out a street map and pinpointed the Vieux Caveau on Rue Bonaparte, just off St. Germain. Okay, where were the nearest places you could get a drink?

Not Gordon Payant's place. It would be closed. Not the Club du Vieux-Colombier, it wouldn't be open yet. The Deux Magots would be open, and so would the Lipp and Flore, but he knew Shell had no credit at any of these popular hangouts, and besides, they wouldn't let anyone as swacked as Shell must be, by this time, hang around.

Bigelow left the suite and headed for the Vieux Caveau. He would just have to start circling around until he found the fellow. Shell wouldn't be wasting what little money he might have on taxis, so he probably hadn't got very far.

Bigelow was right about the St. Germain des Prés cafés. Shell wasn't in any of them, either at a sidewalk table or inside.

But he had one break. Manfred, back on duty as a waiter after his night in uniform as the grand duke he once was, had seen Shell not more than an hour ago. Shell had been staggering, Manfred informed the big cartoonist virtuously. He'd wanted to put a few drinks on the cuff.

"And…?" Bigelow said.

Manfred shrugged hugely. "The management never extends credit to an intoxicated man."

Biggy growled, "I don't suppose you found it in your own goodness of heart to stand him a couple?"

Manfred was haughtly. "I am a former member of the nobility, and at present a waiter. I am not, nor have ever been, a philanthropist."

"Obviously," Biggy growled. "You didn't see what direction Shell headed in, did you?"

"I think he went down Rue Rennes, but I'm not sure. I've never seen Mr. Halliday so intoxicated."

Bigelow Warren had never known Shell to get so drunk, either. He found him, finally, in the Cielito Lindo, a pseudo-Mexican bistro on Rue des Saints-Préres, not far from the Pont du Carrousel.

Shell had a group of eight or ten tourists around and a sketch pad on the table before him. He was swaying in his chair, but it didn't seem to effect the accuracy of his pencil. One by one, he was doing caricatures of the American sightseers.

Currently, he had a red-faced stereotype across from him. Loud sport jacket, two Leica cameras and an exposure meter around his neck, a checkered cap and blue suède shoes. Shell was finishing off the sketch with practiced sweeps of his pencil and the others were looking over his shoulder at the brutal cartoon and laughing hugely.

"Oh, Jesus, that's Harry, all right," one chortled. "Harry, he's got you to a tee."

Harry said, unhappily, "Well, he had *you* to a tee a minute ago. Okay, the drinks are on me."

"Make mine a double tequila, straight," Shell ordered, his voice slurred.

Harry looked down at the sketch. "Hey, that doesn't look anything like me. I'm not *that* fat around the collar."

The others hooted at him.

One of the women shrilled, "Do Mabel. Do Mabel next."

Mabel, another stereotype, wasn't having any. "Not me. Not after what he made *you* look like."

Shell tossed the tequila back. "Who's next?" he slurred. "Do your portrait for a drink."

Harry had picked his up. "Portrait?" he said unhappily. "You call this a portrait? Why, back home I'd sue you for libel."

The rest roared laughter again. "By Jesus, that's Harry, okay. Let me have hold of that and I'll send it to the paper when we get home," one of the men hooted.

Bigelow touched Shell on the shoulder. He looked at the others, and with a motion of his head, requested they go off. Somehow, his mien carried an air of command. Still chuckling or hooting at each other, they drifted over to the bar, four or five with their sketches in their hands, others, unflattered, left the caricatures on the table before Shell.

"Hi, Shell," Bigelow started.

Shell looked up at him woozily. He shook his head. "Hi, Biggy."

"Come on, we're going to the *sauna*," Biggy said. "Over at the Helsinki."

"How come, Biggy? You drunk? Besides, I'm mad at you." He swayed, almost slipping from the chair. "Least, I think I am."

Bigelow took him by the arm. "Come on, Shell. Let's get sobered up. We've got things to talk about."

He picked up the sketch pad, frowned at some of the caricatures on it, then stuck it into his pocket along with the portraits the tourists had abandoned. He took the other by the arm. Shell was too far gone to resist.

"Boy, did I hang one on," he said dismally.

"Sure did," Bigelow agreed. In the back of his head, he was thinking how often he, in exactly this shape, had been hauled out of some familiar bistro by Shell.

He stopped at the bar long enough to inquire for the bill.

"Il n'y a pas addition, Monsieur," he was told. The tourists had paid for Shell's tab in return for his sketches.

Bigelow said wryly, "I should remember this angle for the next time I run out of cash on a pub crawl." Then he added, "If there ever is a next time."

He half supported Shell, half leaned him against a public *pissoir*, while he hailed a cab. He said, "Where'd you pick up that caricature stuff?"

Shell looked at him blearily, "What—"

"Never mind."

A cab came sweeping in, pulled up before them in a Parisian squealing of brakes. Bigelow manhandled Shell into the back, gave directions for the Helsinki Hotel.

"They're going to get a shock when the two of us come in for a *sauna*, with me cold sober and escorting you," he muttered. "They'll probably go out of business, figuring they've seen everything now."

"Wha—?" Shell demanded.

"Nothing. I was being funny."

At the Helsinki, Bigelow growled as he helped the other out of his clothes in preparation for the steam room, "I've always told myself I'd come in here sober someday, just to find out whether or not that overgrown Amazon really gives me a worse going over with that bundle of birch switches than she does anybody else."

He half pushed, half tugged the dazed Shell into the steam room.

* * * *

An hour and a half later, they were relaxed in the same chairs in the Helsinki lobby they'd occupied two days before. Shell was still on the shaky side, but lucid now.

Bigelow didn't attempt to pussyfoot around. He said, "Shell, how do you really feel about Connie at this point?"

Shell looked down at a still-shaking hand and grunted disgust. "How do you mean?" he asked.

"Well, are you still in love with her?"

Shell grimaced and stuck his hands in his pockets so he wouldn't have to look at them. "No," he said. He took a deep breath before going on. "I caught up with reality last night, Biggy. Possibly I haven't thought it all out yet, but the ground work's been done. Connie's out of the past. She's one of the best, but she's not for me. Or me for her. Quite a bit I'm facing up to, besides that. This life isn't for me, either."

Biggy said softly, "Going back to New Elba?"

"And to my father's business?" Shell shook his head. "No. That's not for me, either. I won't be able to stay in Paris. No way of getting work here, what with French legal restrictions. I suppose I'll go back to the States and look around. I'll find my niche, somewhere."

"Listen, Shell," Biggy said, "Connie and I are going to be married."

It would have taken even more than that to have really flustered Shell Halliday at this point.

He nodded his head seriously. "Yes. Yes, that'll be fine. You'll work out swell together. She's a nice guy. So are you, Biggy. If it made any difference at all, I'd apologize for going off my rocker last night. Something just snapped. Too much loaded on at once. Kind of a straw that broke the camel's back."

"It doesn't make any difference," Biggy said. "In fact, it was probably the thing that led Connie and me into seeing we were meant for each other."

Shell shot a prying glance at the big man. Those words sounded slightly on the "square" side to be coming from the supposedly ultra-cynical Biggy. But no, the other wasn't kidding. When you got down to the really important things, they *do* sound not-with-it, because they're simple and completely true without room for cheap cynicism. Biggy and Connie *were* meant for each other, and that was exactly the way to state it.

Shell grinned sourly. "It's going to come as a shock to New Elba social circles. Connie Lockwood goes off to Paris to visit her school days sweetheart and lands the celebrated Bigelow Warren for a husband."

Bigelow was too newly deep in this to see any humorous aspects. "Possibly we could all go back together. Get married in Ohio. You could be my best man."

Shell laughed softly, but shook his head. "That'd wow them, all right, but not for me. I've got New Elba completely out of my blood. It's not that I want to avoid the place—in shame—but it just leaves me cold. Four or five years in Paris makes it a little difficult for me to picture myself going down to the Dairy Maid Drive-in and having a hamburger and malted in the way of a big time."

Biggy raised his eyebrows.

Shell shook his head defensively. "No, I'm not running down small towns, nor hamburgers and malteds. They're fine. But not for me, any more."

"What do you figure on doing, Shell?"

"I don't know, Biggy, but I'm in good health and I've been around more than average. There'll be something."

The big cartoonist pulled the sketch pad and loose caricatures from his side pocket. He leafed through the pages the other had done in the Cielito Lindo and elsewhere. "What's all this?" Biggy asked him.

Shell flushed and reached for the pad, but the other held it away. Shell shrugged and said, "Sometimes, when I'm more than ordinarily broke, I go around the tourist haunts and do portrait sketches for a couple of francs a throw."

"How come I've never seen any of them before? I've seen what you used to do in the name of serious art."

Shell shrugged. "You're an arrived cartoonist, Biggy. This is off-the-cuff stuff, amateur stuff. I'd be like some beginner writer showing his story to Faulkner."

Biggy was looking at a full-length drawing of a Parisian traffic cop. He chuckled. "You call these things portraits? I've never seen such insults. Do they really pay to get raked over the coals like this?"

Shell said uncomfortably. "Sometimes they get mad. However, I sketch 'em the way I see 'em, and usually there's something ludicrous in each person's appearance that sums them up."

Bigelow suddenly brought forth a pencil. "Let's see you do me." He held the pad and pencil to Shell.

"Aw, no. Look, Biggy, I'm pooped. I haven't time for games. I haven't been in bed all night."

"Come on, come on," the big man ordered and shoved the pencil into the other's hand.

Shell decided to get it over with quickly. He squinted at his friend, made a quick curving line, then another. He slashed twice, thrice with the pencil. Did two or three lines of dots. The pencil moved quickly and accurately.

"How long you been doing this stuff?" Biggy wanted to know.

"Ever since I was a kid, really. I always liked caricatures. My mother used to give me the devil."

He finished the cartoon and handed it to Bigelow.

Biggy looked at it and winced. "Oh, would some power the gift give us, to see ourselves as others see us," he misquoted.

"If Bobby Burns could hear that Scottish accent," Shell snorted.

Biggy looked up at him. "Does everybody see me as a guy with a glass perpetually in one hand, in a suit that looks as though it's been slept in?"

"Only those, probably, who know you in Paris."

"Ever do any of these caricatures of current political figures?" Biggy asked suddenly. "You know, de Gaulle, Castro, the President …"

"Sometimes, just for gags or to kill time. What's all this about, Biggy? You working up to offering me a job helping you on the *Bobby* strip? I'm in no mood for further charity."

But the other was shaking his head. "No, Shell. I'm a cold-blooded businessman when it comes to *Bobby* and you're not the type. However, there's something else. Did it ever occur to you that you're a born political cartoonist of the satirical school?"

"No, it never did, and it still doesn't."

"Yep," Biggy said definitely. "And it's no matter of charity. You know the work of Vichy, the Englishman, and David Low, for that matter?"

"Well, sure. They're tops."

Biggy was looking sourly at the sketch Shell had done of him. He winced again and leafed once more through the sketch pad. "And so could you be. I've never seen such a knack for it. Each one of these little things is a masterpiece of character revelation."

Shell shrugged it off again. "I don't know New York. I don't know anything about the field. I wouldn't know how to sell a political cartoon if I knew how to draw one, and I don't."

Biggy shook his head negatively, pushing objections aside. "That's what agents are for. I'll introduce you to mine. Besides that, I've got two or three men on my staff who used to be in the field. They can break you in, show you the ropes. You're a natural."

Shell's mind could hardly move fast enough to encompass all this.

The big man was continuing. "You're probably broke. Fine, I'll stake you to the fare back to the States and put you on my payroll until you're strong enough to stand on your own."

"Hey now, wait a minute. I told you I wasn't interested in charity."

"Neither am I. I told you I was cold-blooded when it came to my business. It wouldn't be charity. In fact, I'd make money out of you. My staff turns out a lot of material besides the daily panel. We produce Sunday strips in color, Hollywood cartoons of *Bobby*, commercial advertising for the magazines with a *Bobby* motif, and a *Bobby* television show is in the making. Then there's a game called *Bobby* and little *Bobby* costumes for kiddies. It's a madhouse. As long as you work in my studio, anything realized from your efforts will go to me. You'll simply be on the payroll. I'll start you at, say, two hundred a week. As soon as you're established, you can go it on your own." He wound it up bluntly. "This is a business proposition, Shell. Say yes, or no."

Shell was slumped in his chair, agape.

"Yes," he managed to get out.

Bigelow hesitated before saying, "We can work out the details later. The cost of your fare back to the States, that sort of thing, we can deduct from your pay. No hurry about it. Meanwhile ..."

The cartoonist dug into his pocket and emerged with some high denomination bills in a money clip. He peeled several of them off. "Meanwhile, you probably have some odds and ends to finish off here in town." He twisted his mouth. "Old Hobbs, over at the Lycée Hotel, claims you owe him a week's rent."

"Yes," Shell said, still trying to assimilate it all. He took the money. "And there's a few other items."

Biggy said, a touch of embarrassment in his voice, "I wonder if you could pull out of the suite tonight, Shell? Sleep somewhere else."

At first Shell didn't get it. Then he reacted with a flush. It was none of his business. "Of course," he said.

The big cartoonist stood up. "I suppose you have a lot to do. We'll be heading for New York as soon as we can get organized. A couple of days, say. Okay?"

"Okay, boss."

Biggy looked at him. "I won't be your boss for long. You'll be on your own in no time at all."

"I think you're right," Shell told him, straight. "I have a feeling you're right."

CHAPTER 9

SHELL SAW CONNIE AGAIN the next morning. He'd sloughed off the last remnants of hangover, both alcoholic and psychic, and was fresh again. In fact, he was more eager for life than he could remember ever having been.

He'd come up for his things, was met at the door by Bigelow who walked him back to the living room, talking about air reservations. The hotel was having a bit of a hassle acquiring them on such short notice.

Connie came out of the bedroom combing her hair, which was down over her shoulders, and humming easily to herself. Her eyes widened when she saw Shell, and then went quickly to Bigelow who smiled encouragingly at her. She wore a negligee.

"Hello, Connie," Shell said uncomfortably.

"Hello, Shelley."

"Excuse me a minute, please," Biggy broke in. "I've got something to do." He left the room.

Connie sat on the couch, her hands in her lap. She said, almost defensively, "Bigelow and I are going to be married, Shelley."

"Yes, he told me. Congratulations are in order to both of you. He's a wonderful guy, Connie."

"Yes." She hesitated. "Shelley, we'll be seeing each other, I imagine, in New York. I think we ought to work things out now."

He shook his head and took one of the chairs across from her. "Nothing to be worked out, Connie. I made a fool of myself and remained one for the best part of five years. I should have called it quits when I first discovered I was no artist. Instead, I managed to hurt everyone concerned."

Now it was she who shook her head. "Spilt milk," she said. "It's silly crying over it. And in the long run, it worked out. I've found Biggy, and we're right for each other. You've found your position. For that matter, even your father and mother will be pleased with your place as a New York political cartoonist."

"Biggy told you about that, eh?"

She nodded. "It sounds wonderful," Connie told him.

He laughed suddenly. "You know, Connie, the old feeling is gone, but I'm still fond of you, and always will be. Don't worry about me in New

York. You can name the first child after me, or something. And I'll be Uncle Shell."

"Hmmm," she said, "that goes only if you promise to name *your* first Bigelow."

He laughed again. "I hadn't thought about that. I suppose I will, sooner or later, wind up with a wife and family, remote as that possibility seems right now."

"How about that Felicity Patterson girl at the party?" she teased.

He grunted negation. "Nice girl, but didn't you hear her announce her engagement to Mike Brett-James?"

"That silly wishy-washy? Don't be ridiculous, Shelley. I know better, being a woman. That girl goes for you, Shelley Halliday. I would have been jealous the other night, had there really been anything true between you and me."

Bigelow came back. He assimilated the air of amiability, grinned bearishly at them both. "How're my two best friends getting along?"

"Friend?" Connie said indignantly. "Is that how you think of *me?*"

Shell and Biggy laughed.

* * * *

Shell Halliday sprawled in his favorite chair, at his favorite table at the Deux Magots and contemplated the scene before him. Tourists and bearded beatniks, artists and Sorbonne students, streetwalkers and expatriate alcoholics, refugees and poets, models and international bums—and even an occasional Frenchman—paraded past. He had a bock before him, a small beer.

To his left was the Abbey, one of the oldest religious buildings in Paris and, in a solid way, one of the most beautiful. Shell wondered idly how many hours he'd spent in its shade in the past five years. Five years? It didn't seem such a long time. This was probably the last time he'd ever sit here at the Deux Magots. Tomorrow, early, they were flying to the States.

In a way, he didn't regret these years in Paris. Who was it—Oscar Wilde or somebody?—who said to deny your past was to commit suicide. No, that wasn't exactly it, but something along that line. There was no use in regretting the past. The thing to do was profit by it. He'd learned a lot about life, here in Paris, and he intended to make use of it.

A girl with a more than usually provocative figure was approaching. Automatically, Shell looked up to her face.

Shirley MacLaine type, he decided all over again. It was Sissy Patterson.

She saw him, too, and hesitated.

Shell twisted his face ruefully and stood up.

"I can recommend the Riesling," he said.

She made a face and came over to him. He held a chair for her.

"I'm leaving this afternoon for London," Sissy told him.

"A drink on me—for once?" he urged.

She shook her head. "A coke, just to keep the waiter happy. I'm cutting out drinking so heavily. It's childish."

Shell ordered the coke. "Now listen for a moment," he said. "You don't have to believe me, but you do owe an accused man the chance to defend himself."

She shrugged impatiently. "If it's about the money, Shell, don't bother. I couldn't care less. And I know just how broke you usually are."

"Look, Sissy. Listen for just a moment. The other night at the party I suddenly remembered how careless you are with your money and your purse. And I realized that gang of people we'd invited up to impress Connie were a bunch of the biggest international bums in Paris. So I went into the bedroom to get your bag and lock it in a bureau drawer. Just as I was proceeding to do that, you walked in, and when you found the bag empty, assumed that I'd done it. The fact is that my fears were evidently justified. Someone at the party pilfered your money before I ever got to it."

"It doesn't make any difference, Shell. Really it doesn't."

He said in irritation, "You don't believe me, do you?"

"Sure I do. Good Heavens, it's not important."

No, she didn't believe him. He wasn't getting through to her. It'd take a bombshell to crack the defensive armor she'd raised to protect herself. And he was all out of bombshells. And there was no way of proving he wasn't just one more slob out for her money. It would be pointless to tell her about the new job.

He gave it up and looked at her. Felicity Patterson, the poor little rich girl. The daughter of the bootlegger who, for all her charm and looks, had no luck with her men. Certainly, she'd never gotten any real love from them.

Well, she was probably right. This time she was playing it smart. She wasn't marrying for love, but for security and position—for herself and her child. How had she introduced Mike the other night? As a viscount. Shell supposed that would immediately make her Lady Brett-James when she married the Britisher. He could see her going back to Palm City, or wherever it was she was from, after a year or two. Lady Brett-James. He had no idea what the better element in Palm City might be like, but he had a suspicion that, like many Americans, they were highly impressed by a title.

And Sissy's love life? Inwardly, Shell shrugged. He imagined that after a time she'd take a lover. It seemed hardly likely that Mike would perform very well in that department, considering his inclinations. Yes, she'd probably take a lover, and when she tired of him, another, and eventually another. But if real love passed her by, at least she'd have what she'd yearned for all her life. Security and position, and a man who hadn't married her for the Patterson fortune.

The fact that he, Shell Halliday, was in love with her was beside the point. If he told her so, tried to convince her that they could make a go of it, what would she think? One more guy on the make. One more man interested in her money, rather than in Sissy Patterson herself.

The coke came and she sipped at it and made a face.

Shell had to laugh.

"Not very strong, is it?" Sissy said, the sides of her mouth drooping.

Actually, she had been evaluating him, too.

In the couple of weeks Sissy had known the easygoing Shell Halliday, she'd formed more than a passing affection for him, and it wasn't only because he was a superior bed companion, one who lived up to her highest demands. There was something in him that offered to the real Sissy more than any man she could remember.

Possibly, it was because Shell made no bones about his way of life. Her husbands had both been phonies, pretending in the early relationship with her that her money made no difference to them. And then, once married, proving that it made all the difference, that it was the real and only thing that counted.

She'd never considered a permanent relationship with Shell, not until that night at Maggie's studio when they'd both been struck by the sudden and powerful awareness of the feeling they had for each other.

And yet, had that sudden welling up of feeling been genuine? Wasn't it merely the after effects of an extremely satisfactory sexual experience?

Did she, or could she, love Shell? Of course. But to what end? Suppose they were married. Immediately, support would fall upon her. They'd live high—on her money. And, finally, what would that lead to? A stepfather Bunny would love and respect? Security and a good home life? No. Never. Eventually, the spontaneity of love, which comes in its first flowering, would fall away and would leave a Shell who knew he was living off a woman, and a Sissy who would know her husband was a parasite.

There was simply no future for them.

Shell said, "So you're going to marry Mike and take off for castles in Scotland and country estates in Ireland."

"That's right." She grinned suddenly. "Can't you just see me, driving the dogcart into town?—the tenants and the locals tipping their hats as I pass?"

Shell twisted his mouth wryly. "I hope it all works out for you, Sissy."

"It will," she said in determination. "I'll *make* it work out." She darted a quick look at her watch and came suddenly to her feet. "I'm going to have to run, Shell. We're leaving shortly. Good luck to you and … Connie."

He didn't bother to tell her about Connie. He stood, too, and held out his hand for a firm shake. "Look, Sissy, you're very high in my books. The highest. I—"

He came to a halt, unable to continue. Then he said, "I wish there could have been something more."

She looked full into his eyes. "I know what you mean. Frankly, I feel the same." She squeezed his hand. "Good luck, Shell." She turned quickly and hurried off, the heels of her shoes going flick, flick, flick.

Shell had no way of knowing that she was crying.

He sat down again and gestured to Maurice for another drink. There went the girl who, though he'd known her for less than two weeks, had meant more to him than any other he could think of—even Connie. Well, so it went.

Dave Shepherd frisked into the chair Sissy had just vacated. He touched Shell on the arm with a fluttering hand. "My dear boy, what a *lovely* party."

"Hello, Dave," Shell said. "Glad you liked it." He would rather have remained alone in this last hour or so in his old haunts, but there was no way of running Dave off without being openly insulting.

"Wasn't that Miss Patterson I just saw?" Dave lisped.

"That's right. Tells me she's off to London this afternoon. She and Mike Brett-James are going to be married."

"*Do* tell. Then that announcement she made at the party wasn't just spoofing? My *dear*, so many people are going to be utterly flabbergasted."

Shell said idly, "Well, Sissy's been through it before. Is this Mike's first marriage?"

"Of *course*," Dave simpered, as though vastly amused.

"It's not as unbelievable as all that," Shell insisted. "What with his titles and all, Mike must be considered quite an eligible bachelor. I'm surprised he lasted this long."

The little homosexual tittered. "My dear boy, you're such an innocent. Over here, they've learned that a title means very little indeed, by itself. Of course, we Americans are so silly about it. When one of our heiresses decides to marry into Continental aristocracy they make no effort to check behind the façade."

Thus far, Shell had been listening without undue concentration. Conversation with Dave Shepherd didn't call for much in the way of attention—it was strictly froth. But something touched him here.

Shell scowled. "What's that got to do with Mike Brett-James? You seemed to suggest that he isn't exactly the richest man in the world," Shell primed.

"*Richest!* My *dear*, he hasn't a shilling to his name."

Shell stared at him. "Are you skidding 'round the bend? His family goes back practically to the cave men. Castles in Scotland, estates in Ireland, all that sort of stuff."

"Oh, don't be ridiculous, dear boy. Do *you* want a castle in Scotland? What in the world would you do with it? Heavens, I know of three or four you could pick up for paying the back taxes."

"But the big estate in Ireland? Big as a cattle ranch."

"Why the Brett-James family doesn't sell that white elephant is a mystery to me." Dave shrugged in his inimitable feminine way. "Probably because they can't find anyone silly enough to buy it. Be your age, Shell dear, castles and country estates are a drug on the market in the British Isles these days. Nobody can afford to keep them up."

"Hi-i-i." Shell let air out of his lungs, realization coming to him. "So Mike hasn't much in the way of money, eh?"

"Shell, dear, I shouldn't be talking like this, I *really* shouldn't, but, you know, Mike *is* rather a bitch. Frankly, he's just as gay as I am, and that's why the family pays him a small remittance to keep out of England."

"Remittance!"

"And *much* too small, believe me." Dave raised his eyebrows and smirked. "Why, Mike is always spending his allowance the first fortnight of the month. Do you know where he's been staying this past week?"

Shell shook his head numbly.

"Well, my dear boy, he's been living with *me*."

"Holy Smoke," Shell said.

Dave said, misinterpreting the other's attitude, "You don't believe me, do you? Well, my dear, let me show you some proof. I found this—" He brought a crumpled letter from an inner pocket and handed it to Shell. "—in my wastebasket, just yesterday. From the earl. You know, Mike's uncle. A title that goes—"

Shell took the letter, turned Dave's voice off, and read. It was on the brief side, but complete. The stationery was crested and ultra-heavy; there was no doubt about authenticity. Evidently, the Brett-James family were delighted with the fact that Michael had met a generous American heiress. Respectably married, there was no reason in the world why dear Michael couldn't return to England. Perhaps, with new financial status, it would be possible to open up the family house in Essex, and everyone could move in.

Shell was on his feet. He hadn't even bothered to finish the note Mike's uncle had written. He had enough.

"See you, Dave," he clipped. He tossed a bill to the table even as he began swivel-hipping his way through the chairs to the sidewalk. "Pay my check for me, will you?" he called over his shoulder.

The cab banged up the Avenue de l'Opéra to Casanova and then skidded left and into the Place Vendome and before the Ritz. Shell tossed money into the driver's lap, muttered for him to donate the change to the Crippled Driver's Fund and dashed for the door.

He remembered her room number. How could he forget?

Shell barged into the room. Mike Brett-James was helping Sissy into her light coat.

Mike looked up and frowned superciliously. "I say, you have a nerve, coming here after the other evening."

Sissy said, puzzled, "Shell! I thought … well, we said our good-byes."

Shell closed the door. "Not exactly," he said to Sissy. He turned to Brett-James. "Let's see the contents of your wallet, Mike, dear boy."

"I *beg* your pardon."

Grinning without humor, Shell stepped quickly forward toward the Englishman, who began to retreat in trepidation.

Shell's foot suddenly lashed out and the tip of his shoe connected with Mike's shinbone. The Englishman howled and stooped to clasp it, hopping on one foot in anguish.

"Shell!" Sissy snapped angrily. "What …?"

Mercilessly, Shell made with what amounted to an uppercut. He could feel nose cartilage yield. Mike, his voice keening a womanlike scream, fell back into a sitting position, his hands to his face now.

Shell had noticed before that the Britisher kept his wallet in his inner coat pocket, rather than on his hip. He stepped forward quickly now, grabbed the other by a lapel, pulled the coat back, and darted a hand in for the pocketbook.

Sissy was wide-eyed. On the face of it, this was straight robbery. Shell was obviously a candidate for the pressure cooker. She didn't know whether to scream, or to make a rush for the phone.

Shell was before her, a wad of money in his hand. "Look, look at this! Recognize it? Francs, pounds, dollars, pesetas. What would this jerk be doing with dollars? How much money did you lose out of your purse, there at the party?"

Her face had gone blank. She took the money Shell held and stared down at it. "But, Mike," she said. "You changed your pesetas at the Spanish-French border, at Port Bou. All of them. I kept ten thousand, thinking I'd be going back to Spain. This is exactly ten thousand."

Mike began blubbering. His nose was bleeding profusely. "You've broken it!" he wailed at Shell.

"I hope so, this time," Shell growled. He spun back to Sissy again. "Look at this letter from the jerk's uncle. Mike's a remittance man, Sissy.

They pay him to stay out of England because he louses up the family reputation. He's as queer as chicken … I mean as a purple cow."

Mike had managed to get to his feet. "Oh, I am not, you cad," he said, his voice high as he dabbed at his nose.

Sissy was regarding him in realization. "Good Heavens, he is, isn't he?" she said. "I wondered why he was so milk-fed in the clinches. I thought maybe he'd warm up after the marriage." She scanned the letter, scowling now.

Shell snapped to Mike, "Beat it, Buster. Sissy and I have important things to discuss."

Shell took him by the arm and hustled him through the door, closing it behind him.

Sissy, hands on hips, was glaring at him. "Good Heavens," she said. "You're awfully uppity."

He approached her, took her two arms in his hands. "Had to be," he grinned. "The cavalry coming to the rescue, that sort of thing. That guy was just one more customer trying to get next to your money. Now look, I just got a job. A pretty good one, and it'll be better. I'll tell you about it later. Meanwhile, you're going to marry me."

"I certainly am not." Her lip began to tremble. "I … it's impossible that Mike's a fake."

"No, it isn't. I'll prove it to you later. No time now. He's queer, too, like I said. Even made a pass at me once. But …" He shook her earnestly. "… that's not important now. What's important is that I'm in love with you. And you're a spoiled brat with too much money, and you know what we're going to do with that fortune you inherited from your old man?"

At the mention of her money, some of the shine went out of Sissy's eyes. "No … what?" she said wearily.

"We're going to put it in a trust fund for Bunny, for when she's of age. You and I aren't going to touch it. We're going to live on my earnings, which means you're going to have to learn to cook and such, my fine woman."

"Good Heavens … we are?"

"Yes. And Bunny's going to be raised like an American kid and she's going to go to American schools. And if she is ever considered a lady, it'll be because of her own sweet self and because you and I have raised her to be one. Not because of some phony title handed down from the Dark Ages."

"Good Heavens," Sissy said.

"Now then," Shell snapped. "Is this what you want?"

"Good Heavens, yes."